the fallen

Book One

Thomas E. Sniegoski

Simon Pulse

NEW YORK LONDON TORONTO SYDNEY SINGAPORE

For Spencer, gone but never forgotten.

And Mulder, the best pally a guy could have.

I'd like to thank my wife and guardian angel (with a pitchfork), LeeAnne, for everything that she does. Without her love and support, the words wouldn't come, so the stories could never be told.

And to Christopher Golden, collaborator and friend, thanks for the gift of confidence when I wasn't quite sure I could pull it off. It is greatly appreciated.

Thanks to the Termination Lisa (Clancy), and her assistant supreme, Lisa Gribbin.

Special thanks are also due to Mom and Dad (for that Catholic upbringing), Eric Powell, Dave Kraus, David Carroll, Dr. Kris Blankenstock and the gang over at Lloyd Animal Medical Center, Tom and Lorie Stanley, Paul Griffin, Tim Cole and the usual suspects, Jon and Flo, Bob and Pat, Don Kramer, John, Jane, Harry and Hugo, Kristy Brandon, and Mike and Anne Murray. An extra-special thanks to Rosalivia Bryant.

prologue

LEBANON, TENNESSEE, 1995

The Tennessee night was screaming.

Eric Powell ran clumsily through the tall grass behind his grandparents' house. He stumbled down the sloping embankment toward the thick patch of swampy woods beyond, hands pressed firmly against his ears.

"I'm not listening," he said through gritted teeth, on the verge of tears. "Stop it. Please! *Shut up.*"

The sounds were deafening, and he wanted nothing more than to escape them. *But where?* The voices were coming from all around.

Eric ran deeper and deeper into the woods. He ran until his lungs felt as if they were on fire, and the beating of his heart was almost loud enough to drown out the sinister warnings from the surrounding darkness.

Almost.

Beneath a weeping willow that had once been a favorite place to escape the stress of teenage life, he stopped to catch his breath. Warily he moved his hands away from his ears and was bombarded with the cacophonous message of the night.

"Danger," warned a tiny, high-pitched squeak from the shadows by the small creek that snaked through the dark wood. *"Danger. Danger. Danger."*

"They come," croaked another. *"They come."*

"Hide yourself," something squawked from within the drooping branches of the willow before taking flight in fear. *"Before it is too late,"* it said as it flew away.

There were others out there in the night, thousands of others all speaking in tongues and cautioning him of the same thing. Something was coming, something bad.

Eric fell back against the tree trying to focus, and his mind flashed back to when he first began to hear the warnings. It had been June 25, of that he was certain. The memory was vividly fresh, for it had been only two months ago and it was not easy to forget one's eighteenth birthday—or the day you begin to lose your mind.

Before that, he heard the world just like any other. The croaking of frogs down by the pond, the angry buzz of a trapped yellow jacket as it threw itself against the screens on the side porch. Common everyday sounds of nature, taken for granted, frequently ignored.

But on his birthday that had changed.

Eric no longer heard them as the sounds of birds chirping or a tomcat's mournful wail in the night. He heard them as voices, voices that exalted in the glory of a beautiful summer's day, voices that spoke of joy as well as sadness, hunger, and fear. At first he tried to block them out, to hear them for what they actually were—just the sounds of animals. But when they began to speak directly to him, Eric came to the difficult realization that he was indeed going insane.

A swarm of fireflies distracted him from his thoughts, their incandescent bodies twinkling in the inky black of the nighttime woods. They dipped and wove in the air before him, their lights communicating a message of grave importance.

"Run," was the missive he read from their flickering bioluminescence. *"Run, for your life is at risk."*

And that is just what he did.

Eric pushed off from the base of the tree and headed toward the gurgling sounds of the tiny creek. He would cross it and head deeper into the woods, so far that no one would ever find him. After all, he had grown up here and doubted there was anyone around who knew the woods better.

But then the question came, the same question that the rational part of his mind had been asking since the warnings began.

What are you afraid of?

The question played over and over in his head as he ran, but he did not know the answer.

Eric jumped the creek. He landed on the other side awkwardly, his sneakered foot sliding across some moss-covered rocks and into the unusually cold water.

The boy gasped as the liquid invaded his shoe, and he scrambled to remove it from the creek's numbing embrace. Its chilling touch spurring him to move faster. He ducked beneath the low-hanging branches of young trees that grew along the banks of the miniature river, then he plunged deeper into the wilderness.

But what are you running from? a rational voice asked, not from the woods around him but from his own mind. His own voice, a calm voice, that sought to override his sense of panic. This voice wanted him to stop and confront his fears, to see them for what they really were. *There is no danger,* said the sensible voice. *There is nobody chasing you, watching you.*

Eric slowed his pace.

"Keep running," urged something as it slithered beneath an overturned stump, its shiny scales reflecting the starlight.

And he almost listened to the small, hissing voice, almost sped up again. But then Eric shook his head and began to walk. Others called to him from the bushes, from the air above his head, from the grass beneath his feet, all urging him to flee, to run like a crazy person, which was exactly what he decided he was.

At that moment, Eric made a decision. He wasn't going to listen to them anymore. He wasn't going to run from some invisible threat. He was going to turn around, go back to his grandparents' home, wake them up, and explain what was happening. He would tell them that he needed help, that he needed to get to a hospital right away.

His mind made up, Eric stopped in a clearing and looked up into the early-morning sky. A thick patch of gray clouds that reminded him of steel wool slowly rubbed across the face of a radiant moon. He didn't want to hurt his grandparents. They had already been through so much. His mother, their daughter, pregnant and unwed, died giving birth to him. They raised him as if he were their own, giving him all the love and support he could have ever hoped for. And how would he repay them? With more sadness.

Scalding tears flooded his eyes as he imagined what it would be like when he returned to the house and roused the poor elderly couple from sleep. He could see their sad looks of disappointment as he explained that he was hearing voices—that he was nineteen years old and losing his mind.

And as if in agreement, the voices of the night again came to life: chattering, wheezing, tremulous, quavering, gargling life.

"Run, run," they said as one. *"Run for your life, for they have arrived!"*

Eric looked around him; the ruckus was deafening. Since his bout with madness began, never had the voices been this loud, this frantic. Maybe they suspected he was coming to his senses. Maybe they knew that their time with him would soon be ending.

"They are here! Flee! Hide yourself! It is not too late. Run!"

He spun around, fists clenched in angry resignation. "No more!" he yelled to the trees. "I'm not going to listen to you anymore," he added to the air above his head and the earth beneath his feet. "Do you understand me?" he asked the darkness that encircled the clearing.

Eric turned in a slow circle, his insanity still attempting to overwhelm him with its clamorous jabber. He could stand it no more.

"Shut up!" he shrieked at the top of his lungs. "Shut up! Shut up! Shut up!"

And all went instantly quiet.

As intolerable as the voices had become, the sudden lack of them was equally extreme. There was nothing now: no buzz of insects, no cries of night birds. Not even leaves rustled by the wind. The silence was deafening.

"Well, all right then," he said, speaking

aloud again to make sure that he hadn't gone deaf. Made uneasy by the abrupt hush, he turned to leave the small clearing the way he had entered.

Eric stopped short. A lone figure stood on the path.

Was it a trick of the shadows? The woods, darkness, and moonlight conspiring to drive him crazier than he already was? Eric closed his eyes and opened them again trying to focus on the manlike shape. It still appeared to be somebody blocking his way.

"Hello?" He moved tentatively closer to the dark figure. "Who's there?" Eric still could not make out any details of the stranger.

The shape came toward him, and so did the darkness, as if the undulating shadows that clung to the figure were part of his makeup. The comical image of Pig Pen from the *Charlie Brown* cartoons, surrounded by his ever present cloud of dust and dirt, quickly flashed across Eric's mind's eye. In a perverse way it did kind of remind him of that, only this was far more unnerving.

Eric quickly stepped back.

"Who is it?" he asked, his voice higher with fear. He had always hated how his voice sounded when he was afraid. "Don't come any closer," he warned, making a conscious effort to bring the pitch down to sound more threatening.

The figure cloaked in darkness stopped in its

tracks. Even this much farther into the clearing, Eric could not discern any features. He was beginning to wonder if his psychosis had started to play games with him, this shadow being nothing more than a creation of his insanity.

"Are . . . are you real?" Eric stammered.

It was as if he had screamed the question, the wood was still so unusually silent.

The darkness in the shape of a man just stood there and Eric became convinced of its unreality. *Yet another symptom of the breakdown,* he thought with a disgusted shake of his head. *It couldn't stop with hearing voices,* he chided himself, *oh no, now I have to see things.*

"Guess that answers that question," Eric said aloud as he glared at the figment of his dementia. "What's the matter?" he asked. "Miss your cue or something? When I realize you're nothing but crazy bullshit my mind made up, you're supposed to disappear." He waved the shape away. "Go. I know I'm nuts, you don't need to prove it. Beat it."

The figure did not move, but the covering of shadows that hugged it did. The darkness seemed to open. Like the petals of some night-blooming flower, the ebony black peeled away to reveal a man within.

Eric studied the man, searching his memory for some glimmer of recognition, but came away with nothing. He was tall, at least six feet, and thin, dressed in a black turtleneck, slacks.

And despite the rather muggy temperature, he noticed the man was wearing a gray trench coat.

The man seemed to be studying him as well, tilting his head from one side to the other. His skin was incredibly pale, almost white. His hair, which was worn very long and severely combed back, was practically the same color. Eric had gone to elementary school with a girl who looked like that; her name was Cheryl Baggley and she, too, had been albino.

"I know this is going to sound crazy," Eric said to the man, "but . . ." he stammered as he tried to formulate the most sane way to ask the question. "You are real . . . right?"

The man did not respond at once. As the mysterious stranger pondered the question, Eric noticed his eyes. The oily shadow that had cocooned him previously seemed to have pooled in his eye sockets. He had never seen eyes as deep and dark as these.

"Yes," the pale-skinned man said curtly, his voice sounding more like the caw of a crow.

Startled, Eric didn't grasp the meaning of the man's sudden reply and stared at him, confused. "Yes? I don't . . ." He shook his head nervously.

"Yes," the man again responded. "I am real." He emphasized each of the words as he spoke them.

His voice was strange, Eric thought, as if he were not comfortable speaking the language.

"Oh . . . good, that's good to know. Who are

you? Were you sent to find me?" he questioned. "Did my grandparents call the police? I'm really sorry you had to come all the way out here. As you can see, I'm fine. I'm just dealing with some stuff and . . . well, I just need to get back to the house and have a long talk with . . ."

The man stiffly held up a pale hand. "The sound of you, it offends me," he said, a snarl upon his lips. "Abomination, I command you to be silent."

Eric started as if slapped. "Did . . . did you just call me an abomination?" he asked, confusion and fear raising the pitch of his voice again.

"There are few words in this tongue that define the likes of you better," growled the stranger. "You are a blight upon His favored world, an abhorrence in the eyes of God—but you are not the one that incites me so." The hand held out to silence the boy was turned palm up. Something had begun to glow in its ghostly pale center. "However, that does not change the reality that you must be smited."

Eric felt the hair at the back of his neck stand on end, the flesh on his arms erupt in tingling gooseflesh. He didn't need the voices of the wood to warn him that something was wrong; he could feel it in the forest air.

He turned to run, to hurl himself through the thick underbrush. He had to get away. Every fiber of his being screamed danger, and he allowed the primitive survival mechanism of flight to overtake him.

Four figures suddenly blocked his way, each attired as the stranger, each with a complexion as pale as the face of the full moon above. *How is this possible?* His mind raced. How could four people sneak up on him without making a sound?

Something whined at the newcomers' feet, and he saw a young boy crouched there. He was filthy, naked, his hair long and unkempt, a thick string of snot dripping down from one nostril to cling to his dirty lip. The boy's expression told Eric that there was something wrong with him—that he was touched in some way. And then he noticed the leather collar that encircled the child's neck, and the leash that led to the hand of one of the strangers, and Eric knew something was very wrong indeed.

The boy began to strain upon the leash, pointing a dirt-encrusted finger at him, whining and grunting like an animal.

The strangers fixed their gazes upon Eric with eyes of solid shadow and began to spread out, eliminating any chance of escape. The wild boy continued to jabber.

Eric whipped around to see that the other figure had come closer. His hand was still outstretched before him—but now it was aflame.

His mind tried to process this event. There

was a fire burning in the palm of the man's hand, and the most disturbing thing was, it didn't seem to bother him in the least.

Eric felt his legs begin to tremble as the orange-and-yellow flame grew, leaping hungrily into the air. The stranger moved steadily closer. Eric wanted to run screaming, to lash out and escape those who corralled him, but something told him it would be for naught.

Fear overcame him and he fell to his knees, feeling the cold dampness begin to soak through his pants. There was no reason for him to turn around; the feral child growled at his back and he knew the four strangers now moved to flank him. He kept his gaze on the man standing above him holding fire in the palm of his hand.

"Who are you?" the boy asked dully, mesmerized by the miraculous flame, which appeared to be taking on the shape of something else entirely.

The stranger looked upon him with eyes black and glistening, his expression void of any emotion. Eric could see himself reflected in their inky surface.

"Why are you doing this?" he asked pathetically.

The stranger cocked his head oddly. Eric could feel the heat of the flame upon his upturned face.

"What was it the monkey apostle Matthew scribbled about us in one of his silly little books?" the man asked no one in particular. "'The Son of Man shall send them forth, and they shall gather out of His kingdom all things that offend, and those who do evil, and shall cast them into a furnace of fire.' Or something to that effect," he added with a horrible grin.

Eric had never seen anything more unnatural. It was as if the stranger's face lacked the proper musculature to complete the most common of human expressions.

"I don't understand," he said in a voice nearly a whisper.

The man moved the flaming object from one hand to the other, and Eric followed it with his eyes. The fire had become a sword.

A flaming sword.

"It is better that you do not," the man said, raising the burning blade above his head.

The boy watched the weapon of fire descend, his face upturned as if to seek the rays of the rising sun. And then all that he was, and all that he might have become, was consumed in fire.

chapter one

Aaron Corbet was having the dream again.

Yet it was so much more than that.

Since they began, over three months before, the visions of sleep had grown more and more intense—more vivid. Almost real.

He is making his way through the primitive city, an ancient place constructed of brown brick, mud, and hay. The people here are in a panic, for something attacks their homes. They run about frenzied, their frightened cries echoing throughout the cool night. Sounds of violence fill the air, blades clanging together in battle, the moans of the wounded—and something else he can't quite place, a strange sound in the distance, but moving closer.

Other nights he has tried to stop the frightened citizens, to catch their attention, to ask them what is happening, but they do not see or hear him. He is a ghost to their turmoil.

Husbands and wives, shielding small children between them, scramble across sand-covered streets desperately searching for shelter. Again he listens to their fear-filled voices. He does not understand their language, but the meaning is quite clear. Their lives and the lives of their children are in danger.

For nights too numerous to count he has come to this place, to this sad village and witnessed the panic of its people. But not once has he seen the source of their terror.

He moves through the winding streets of the dream place, feeling the roughness of desert sand beneath his bare feet. Every night this city under siege becomes more real to him, and tonight he feels its fear as if it were his own. And again he asks himself, fear of what? Who are they who can bring such terror to these simple people?

In the marketplace a boy dressed in rags, no older than he, darts out from beneath a tarp covering a large pile of yellow, gourdlike fruit. He watches the boy stealthily travel across the deserted market, sticking close to the shadows. The boy nervously watches the sky as he runs.

Odd that the boy would be so concerned with the sky overhead.

The boy stops at the edge of the market and crouches within a thick pool of night. He stares longingly across the expanse of open ground at another area of darkness on the other side.

There is unrelenting fear on the dark-skinned youth's face; his eyes are wide and white. What is he so afraid of? *Aaron looks up himself and sees only the night, like velvet adorned with twinkling jewels. There is nothing to fear there, only beauty to admire.*

The boy darts from his hiding place and scrambles across the open area. He is halfway there when the winds begin. Sudden, powerful gusts that come out of nowhere, hurling sand, dirt, and dust.

The boy stops short and shields his face from the scouring particles. He is blinded, unsure of his direction. Aaron wants to call to him, to help the boy escape the mysterious sandstorm, but knows that his attempts would be futile, that he is only an observer.

And there is the sound. He can't place it exactly, but knows it is familiar. There is something in the sky above—something that beats at the air, stirring the winds, creating the sudden storm.

The boy is screaming. His sweat-dampened body is powdered almost white in a sheen of fine dust and desert sand.

The sounds are louder now, closer.

What is that? *The answer is right at the edge of his knowing. He again looks up into the sky. The sand still flies about, tossed by the winds. It stings his face and eyes, but he has to see—he has to know what makes these strange pounding sounds, what creates gusts of wind powerful enough to propel sand and rock. He has to know the source of such unbridled horror in these people of the dream-city—in this boy.*

And through the clouds of fine debris, he sees them. For the first time he sees them.

They are wearing armor. Golden armor that glistens in the dancing light thrown from the flames of their weapons.

The boy runs toward him. It seems that Aaron is suddenly visible. The boy reaches out, pleading to be saved in the language of his people.

This time, he understands every word. He tries to answer, but earsplitting shrieks fill the night, the excited cries of predators that have discovered their prey.

The boy tries to run, but there are too many.

Aaron can do nothing but watch as the birdlike creatures descend from the sky, falling upon the boy, his plaintive screams of terror drowned out by the beating of powerful wings.

Angels' wings.

LYNN, MASSACHUSETTS

It was Gabriel's powerful, bed-shaking sneeze that pulled Aaron from the dream and back to the waking world.

Aaron's eyes snapped open as another explosion of moisture dappled his face. For the moment, the dream was forgotten and all that occupied his mind was the attentions of an eighty-pound Labrador retriever named Gabriel.

"Unnngh," he moaned as he pulled his arm up from the warmth beneath the covers to wipe away the newest spattering of dog spittle.

"Thanks, Gabe," he said, his voice husky

from sleep. "What time is it anyway? Time to get up?" he asked the dog lying beside him.

The yellow retriever leaned its blocky head forward to lick the back of his exposed hand, his muscular bulk blocking Aaron's view of the alarm clock.

"Okay, okay," Aaron said as he pulled his other hand out to ruffle the dog's velvety soft, golden-brown ears, and wiggled himself into an upright position to check the time.

Craving more attention, Gabriel flipped over onto his back and swatted at Aaron with his front paws. He chuckled and rubbed the dog's exposed belly before training his eyes on the clock on the nightstand beside his bed.

Aaron watched the red digital readout change from 7:28 to 7:29.

"Shit," he hissed.

Sensing alarm in his master, Gabriel rolled from his back to his stomach with a rumbling bark.

Aaron struggled from the bed, whipped into a frenzy by the lateness of the hour.

"Shit. Shit. Shit. Shit," he repeated as he pulled off his Dave Matthews concert T-shirt and threw it onto a pile of dirty clothes in the corner of the room. He pulled down his sweat-pants and kicked them into the same general vicinity. He was late. Very late.

He'd been studying for Mr. Arslanian's history exam last night, and his head was so crammed with minutiae about the Civil War that he must have forgotten to set the alarm. He had less than a half hour to get to Kenneth Curtis High School before first bell.

Aaron lunged for his dresser and yanked clean underwear and socks from the second drawer. In the mirror above, he could see Gabriel curiously staring at him from the bed.

"Man's best friend, my butt," he said to the dog on his way into the bathroom. "How could you let me oversleep?"

Gabriel just fell to his side among the tousled bedclothes and sighed heavily.

Aaron managed to shower, brush his teeth, and get dressed in a little more than seventeen minutes.

I might be able to pull this off yet, he thought as he bounded down the stairs, loaded bookbag slung over his shoulder. If he got out the door right at this moment and managed to make all the lights heading down North Common, he could probably pull into the parking lot just as the last bell rang.

It would be close, but it was the only option he had.

In the hallway he grabbed his jacket from the coatrack and was about to open the door when he felt Gabriel's eyes upon him.

The dog stood behind him, watching him intensely, head cocked at a quizzical angle that said, "Haven't you forgotten something?"

Aaron sighed. The dog needed to be fed and taken out to do his morning business. Normally he would have had more than enough time to see to his best friend's needs, but today was another story.

"I can't, Gabe," he said as he turned the doorknob. "Lori will give you breakfast and take you out."

And then it hit him. He'd been in such a hurry to get out of the house that he hadn't noticed his foster mother's absence.

"Lori?" he called as he stepped away from the door and quickly made his way down the hall to the kitchen. Gabriel followed close at his heels.

This is odd, he thought. Lori was usually the first to rise in the Stanley household. She would get up around five A.M., get the coffee brewing, and make her husband, Tom, a bag lunch so he could be out of the house and to the General Electric plant where he was a foreman, by seven sharp.

The kitchen was empty, and with a hungry Gabriel by his side, Aaron made his way through the dining room to the living room.

The room was dark, the shades on the four windows still drawn. The television was on, but had gone to static. His seven-year-old foster brother, Stevie, sat before the twenty-two-inch screen, staring as if watching the most amazing television program ever produced.

Across the room, below a wall of family photos that had jokingly become known as the wall of shame, his foster mom was asleep in a leather recliner. Aaron was disturbed at how old she looked, slumped in the chair, wrapped in a worn, navy blue terry cloth robe. It was the first time he ever really thought about her growing older, and that there would be a day when she wouldn't be around anymore. *Where the hell did that come from?* he wondered. He pushed the strange and really depressing train of thought away and attempted to think of something more pleasant.

When the Stanleys had taken him into their home as a foster child, it had been his seventh placement since birth. What was it that the case-workers used to say about him? "He's not a bad kid, just a bit of an introvert with a bad temper." Aaron smiled. He never expected the placements to last, and had imagined that there would be an eighth, ninth, and probably even a hundredth placement before he was cut loose from the foster care system and let out into the world on his own.

A warm pang of emotion flowed through him as he remembered the care this woman and her husband had given him over the years. No matter how he misbehaved, or acted out, they stuck with him, investing their time, their energy, and most importantly, their love. The Stanleys weren't just collecting a check from the state; they really cared about him, and eventually he came to think of them as the parents he never knew.

Gabriel had wandered over to the boy in front of the television and was licking his face—Aaron knew it was only to catch the residue of the child's breakfast. But the boy did not respond, continuing to stare at the static on the screen, eyes wide, mouth agape.

Steven was the Stanleys' only biological child and he had autism, the often misunderstood mental condition that left those afflicted so absorbed with their own reality, that they were rarely able to interact with the world around them. The boy could be quite a handful and Lori stayed home to care for his special needs.

Lori twitched and came awake with a start. "Stevie?" she asked groggily, looking for her young son.

"He's watching his favorite show," Aaron said, indicating Gabriel and the little boy. He looked back to his foster mom. "You all right?"

Lori stretched and, pulling her robe tight around her throat, smiled at him. Her smile had always made him feel special and this morning wasn't any different. "I'm fine, hon, just a little tired is all." She motioned with her chin to the boy in front of the television. "He had a bad night and the static was the only thing that calmed him down."

She glanced over at the mini–grandfather clock hanging on the wall and squinted. "Is that the time?" she asked. "What are you still doing here? You're going to be late for school."

He started to explain as she sprang from the seat and began to push him from the room. "I was up late studying and forgot to set the alarm and . . ."

"Tell me later," she said as she placed the palm of her hand in the small of his back, helping him along.

"Would you mind feeding—"

"No, I wouldn't, and I'll take him for a walk," Lori said, cutting him off. "Get to school and ace that history test."

He was halfway out the door when he heard her call his name from the kitchen. There was a hint of panic in her voice.

Aaron poked his head back in.

"I almost forgot," she said, the dog's bowl in one hand and a cup of dry food in the other. Gabriel stood attentively at her side, drool streaming from his mouth to form a shiny puddle at his paws.

"What is it?" he asked, a touch of impatience beginning to find its way into his tone.

She smiled. "Happy birthday," she said, and pursed her lips in a long distance kiss. "Have a great day."

My birthday, he thought closing the door behind him and running to his car.

With all the rushing about this morning, he'd forgotten.

† † †

Aaron squeaked into homeroom just as the day's announcements were being read over the school's ancient PA system.

Mrs. Mihos, the elderly head of the math department mere months away from retirement, looked up from her copy of *Family Circle* and gave him an icy stare.

He mouthed the words "I'm sorry" and quickly found his seat. He had learned that the less said to Mrs. Mihos the better. Her edicts were simple: Be on time to homeroom, turn in notes to explain absences in a timely fashion, and whatever you do, don't be a wiseass. Aaron chillingly recalled how Tommy Philips, now seated at the back of the classroom intently keeping his mouth shut, had attempted to be the funny guy. He'd written a joke letter to explain an absence, and found himself with a week's worth of detentions. There was nothing the math teacher hated more than a wiseass.

Aaron chanced a look at the old woman and saw that she was flipping through the attendance sheets to change his status from absent to present. He breathed a sigh of relief as the first period bell began to ring. *Maybe today wouldn't be a total disaster after all.*

First period American Literature went fine, but halfway through second period, while taking Mr. Arslanian's test, Aaron decided that he couldn't have been more wrong about the day.

Not only was he blanking on some of the information he had studied, but he also had one of the worst headaches he could ever remember. His head felt as if it were vibrating, buzzing like someone had left an electric shaver running inside his skull. He rubbed at his brow furiously and tried to focus on an essay question about the social and political ramifications of the Richmond Bread Riot. Arslanian's fascination with obscure events of the Civil War was going to give him an aneurysm.

The remainder of the class passed in the blink of an eye, and Aaron wondered if he had passed out or maybe even been taken by space aliens. He had barely finished the last of the essay questions when the end-of-period bell clanged, a real plus for the pain in his head. He quickly glanced over the pages of his test. It wasn't the best he'd ever done, but considering how he felt, he didn't think it was too bad.

"I'd like to give you another couple of hours to wrap the test up in a pretty pink bow, Mr. Corbet . . ."

Aaron had zoned out again. He looked up to see the heavyset form of Mr. Arslanian standing beside his desk, hand beckoning.

"But my wife made a killer turkey for dinner last night and I have leftovers waiting for me in the teachers' lounge."

Aaron just stared, the annoying buzz in his head growing louder and more painful.

"Your exam, Mr. Corbet," demanded Mr. Arslanian.

Aaron pulled himself together and handed the test to his teacher. Then he gathered up his books and prepared to leave. As he stood the room began to spin and he held on to the desk for a moment, just in case.

"Are you all right, Mr. Corbet?" Arslanian asked as he ambled back to his desk. "You look a little pale."

Aaron was amazed that he only looked pale. He imagined there should have been blood shooting out his ears and squirting from his nostrils. He was feeling that bad. "Headache," he managed on his way to the door.

"Take some Tylenol," the teacher called after him, "and a cold rag on your head. That's what works for me."

Always a big help, that Mr. Arslanian, Aaron thought as he stepped lightly in an effort to keep his skull from breaking apart and decorating the walls with gore.

The hallway was jammed with bodies coming, going, or just hanging out in small packs in front of brightly colored lockers, catching up on the freshest gossip. *It's amazing,* Aaron thought sarcastically, *how much dirt can happen during one fifty-minute period.*

Aaron moved through the flow of students. He would drop off his books, and then go to the nurse's office to get something for his headache.

It was getting worse, like listening to the static of an untuned radio playing inside his brain.

As he maneuvered around the pockets of people, he exchanged an occasional smile or a nod of recognition, but the few who acknowledged him were only being polite. He knew people looked at him as the quiet, loner guy with the troubled past, and he did very little to dispel their notions of him. Aaron didn't have any real friends at Ken Curtis, merely acquaintances, and it didn't bother him in the least.

He finally reached his locker and began to dial the combination.

Maybe if he got something into his stomach he'd feel better, he thought, remembering that he hadn't eaten anything since the night before. He swung the locker door open and began to unload his books.

A girl laughed nearby. He looked behind him to see Vilma Santiago at her locker with three of her friends. They were staring in his direction, but quickly looked away and giggled conspiratorially. *What's so funny?* he wondered.

They were speaking loudly enough for him to hear them. The only problem was they were speaking Portuguese, and he had no idea what they were saying. Two years of French did him little good while eavesdropping on Brazilian girls' conversations.

Vilma was one of the most beautiful girls he had ever seen. She had transferred to Ken Curtis last year from Brazil, and within months had become one of the school's top students. Smart as well as gorgeous, a dangerous combination, and one that had left him smitten. They saw each other at their lockers every day, but had never really spoken. It wasn't that he didn't want to speak to her, just that he could never think of anything to say.

He turned to arrange the books in his locker, and again felt their eyes upon him. They were whispering now, and he could feel his paranoia swell.

"Ele nâo é nada feio. Que bunda!"

The pain in his head was suddenly blinding, as if somebody had taken an ice pick and plunged it into the top of his skull. The feeling was excruciating and he almost cried out—certain to have provided his audience with a few good laughs. He pressed his forehead against the cool metal of the locker and prayed for respite. *It can't hurt this bad for very long,* he hoped. As the hissing grew more and more intense, shards of broken glass rubbed into his brain. He thought he would pass out as strange colorful patterns blossomed before his eyes and the pain continued to build.

The torturous buzzing came to an explosive climax, circuits within his mind suddenly overloaded, and before he fell unconscious—it was gone. Aaron stood perfectly still, waiting, afraid that if he moved the agony would return. *What was that all about?* he wondered, his hand coming up to his nose to check for bleeding.

There was nothing. No pain, no blaring white noise. In fact, he felt better than he had all morning. *Maybe this is just part of a bizarre biological process one goes through when turning eighteen,* he thought, bemused, reminding himself again that it was his birthday.

As he slammed the locker door, he realized that Vilma and her friends were still talking. "Estou cansada de pizza. Semana passada, nós comemos pizza, quase todo dia." They were discussing lunch options—cafeteria versus going off campus for pizza. Vilma wanted to go to the cafeteria, but the others were pressing for the pizza.

Aaron turned away from his locker considering whether or not he should still see the nurse, and caught Vilma's eye. She smiled shyly and quickly averted her gaze.

But not before the others noticed and began to tease her mercilessly. "Porqué? Vocé está pensando que una certo persoa vai estar no refeitó rio hoje?" Did she want to eat in the cafeteria because of a certain boy standing nearby? they asked her.

Aaron felt himself break out in a cold sweat. His suspicion was justified, for in fact the girls were talking about him.

"É, e daí? Eu acho que ele é un tesâo." Vilma responded to her friends' taunts and glanced again in his direction.

They were all looking at him when it dawned. He knew what they were saying. Vilma and her friends *were* still speaking to one another in Portuguese—but somehow he could understand each and every word.

But the most startling thing was what Vilma had said.

"Eu acho que ele é un tesâo."

She said he was cute.

Vilma Santiago thought he was cute!

chapter two

At the back of the West Lynn Veterinary Hospital, where Aaron worked after school, a greyhound named Hunter sniffed a patch of yellowed grass with great interest.

"Someone you know?" Aaron asked the brindle-colored dog as he reached out to affectionately scratch him just above his long, whiplike tail.

The dog slowly turned his long neck and wagged his tail in response, before another scent hidden elsewhere in the grass diverted his attention.

Aaron glanced at his watch. It was a little after eight thirty, and he was exhausted. He was hoping that Hunter, who had been constipated since undergoing a procedure to remove a tennis ball from his large intestine, would finally get around to doing his thing so Aaron could go home, have something to eat, and do some schoolwork before passing out.

The dog pulled him into a patch of shadow, nose practically pressed to the ground, turned in a circle and finally did his business.

"Happy birthday to me," Aaron muttered, looking up into the twilight sky. "Somebody up there must like me."

He dragged the greyhound back to the animal hospital, his mind reviewing the strangeness of the day. The business at his locker with Vilma and her friends crept back into his consciousness, and he felt a queasy sensation blossom in the pit of his stomach.

Had he been mistaken? he wondered as he pulled open the door. Had they suddenly switched to English from Portuguese? *No,* he thought, *no, I was definitely hearing Portuguese—and understanding it. But how is that possible?*

Hunter pranced into the cheerfully decorated lobby, his toenails happily clicking on the slick tile floor like tap shoes, excited to see Michelle, the veterinary assistant, standing there.

"So," she asked the big dog, hands on her hips, "did we have success?"

She stroked the dog's pointy snout and rubbed at his ears. The dog was in heaven as it pressed itself against her and gazed up lovingly.

"Well?" she asked again.

Aaron realized she was no longer speaking

to the dog, and emerged from his thoughts.

"Sorry," he said. "Yes, the mission was a complete and total success. We'll probably need some heavy construction equipment to clean up after him, but he did what he had to do."

Michelle wrinkled her nose as she went around the corner of the reception desk. "Yuck. Remind me not to go out back for a while." She pulled a folder from a wall rack behind her and opened it. "I'll make a note for Dr. Kris, and our long-legged friend should be sprung tomorrow."

Aaron barely heard the girl, who was as close to a friend as he'd ever had. He was again lost in his thoughts about the impossibility of what had happened at school. There had to be a rational explanation. Maybe it had something to do with his headache.

"Earth to Corbet," he heard the girl say. Her hands covered her mouth to make it sound as though her voice were coming over a loud-speaker. "This is mission control, over. It appears that one of our astronauts is missing."

Aaron smiled and shook his head. "Sorry. It's been a long day and I'm wiped."

She smiled back and returned the folder to the rack on the wall. "It's cool. Just bustin' yuh," she said, pulling her colorfully dyed, shoulder-length hair away from her face. "Bad day at school or what?"

The two had started working at the clinic around the same time and got along quite well.

Michelle had said that he reminded her of a boyfriend she'd once had: tall, dark, and brooding, the first of many to break her heart. She was older than he by five years, and explained often that her high school days were some of her most painful, so she fancied herself an expert on teen angst.

"You remember how it was, old lady," he said with a laugh that she reciprocated. "Let me get Hunter back into his cage so we can get out of here."

He hauled the greyhound out from around the counter, where he had been sniffing around a wastepaper basket, and toward the doors to the kennels in the back.

"Hey, Aaron," Michelle called after him.

He turned. "What do you want now?"

For a moment she seemed to be studying him. "You sure you're okay? Anything you want to talk about?"

The idea of sharing the bizarreness of his day was tempting, but he decided against it. The last thing he needed was Michelle thinking that not only was he "dark and brooding," but the equally appealing "psychotic" as well.

"I'm fine, really," he assured her. "Just tired is all."

He pushed through the door and led the greyhound to the kennel. It was a large room filled with cages of all sizes, big cages for the larger breeds and tiny cages for what Dr. Bufman lovingly referred to as the rat dogs. Aaron returned Hunter to his current accommodations, said hello to the other dogs, then went to the staff area where he kept his things. He removed his blue work smock, hung it on a hanger, and put on his street shirt.

He was so tired he felt as though he were moving in slow motion. *Is this what it's like to get old? Just imagine what it'll feel like to be thirty,* he thought. He slung his bookbag over his shoulder and forced himself back through the kennel toward the lobby door, looking at his watch again. It was a quarter to nine. If he made it home by nine, had a quick bite and did the bare minimum on his assignments, maybe he could be in bed by ten thirty. Sleep: It sounded like a plan.

The image of a dark-skinned boy being viciously torn apart by angels appeared before his eyes, and he jumped, startled by the sudden flash of recollection.

Maybe I'll just skip the homework and get right to bed, he thought, a bit unnerved by the dream flashback. *Give the brain a chance to rest.*

He reached the lobby and as he rounded the reception desk, noticed a woman standing there with a German shepherd puppy at her heels. Michelle had a file in her hand and looked at him. From the expression on her face he had no doubt she was annoyed.

"This is Mrs. Dexter," she said, hitting the

edge of the folder on the open palm of her hand. "Sheba is being spayed first thing in the morning. Mrs. Dexter was supposed to bring Sheba earlier but forgot."

Aaron closed his eyes for a moment and sighed. He could see his hopes of getting to bed at a reasonable time slipping away.

"I'm so sorry," Mrs. Dexter began. "I completely lost track of time and . . ." The dog had begun to sniff around the floor, straining against her leash, practically pulling the woman off balance.

Aaron stopped listening to the woman's excuses and set his bag down on the floor. He reached across the desk and took the folder from Michelle.

"You get out of here. I'll take care of this," he said.

"Are you sure?" Michelle asked, already taking her purse from the back of a chair. "I could stay a little longer but I've got this thing tonight and . . ."

Aaron shook his head. "I got it. Get out of here. You can owe me."

Michelle smiled briefly and moved around the counter. "Thanks, Aaron. Everything you need should be right there. Have a good night."

He waved as she went out the door, then returned his attention to the open folder. "Okay," he said, removing some papers from inside. "Fill these out for me, please."

Mrs. Dexter took the forms. She let go of the leash and let her dog explore the open lobby. "I'm really sorry about this," she said as she removed a pair of glasses from her purse and put them on. "I was hoping there'd still be someone here." She began to fill out the first form. "Lucky you, huh?"

Sheba approached him cautiously, tail wagging, ears back.

"Lucky me," he agreed as he held out his hand for the young dog to sniff. She licked it and he began to pat her.

It took twenty minutes for Mrs. Dexter to complete the appropriate paperwork and be on her way.

"Sheba will be fine," he reassured the teary-eyed owner as he opened the door to let her out. "The doctor will do her surgery first thing in the morning. You can call around noontime to find out how she did and when she can go home."

The woman squatted in the doorway and gave her dog a last hug and a kiss on the head.

"Thanks for everything," she said as she stood. "I'm sorry for keeping you so late."

Aaron felt a twinge of guilt. It was hard to be annoyed with anyone who showed so much love for a pet.

Sheba began to whine as she watched her master getting into the minivan without her.

"It's all right, girl," Aaron said as he gently tugged on the leash. "Let's get you set up for the night. We've got some lovely accommodations, and you certainly won't be lonely."

He led her through to the kennel. The smells of the other dogs must have been overwhelming, for she tucked her tail between her trembling legs and backed up against him.

"It's okay," he assured her—just as all hell broke loose.

Every dog in the kennel began to go wild, barking crazily, lunging at the doors to their cages, digging furiously with their paws.

Sheba backed up even farther. She looked up at him nervously and then back to the misbehaving canines, as if to say, "What the hell's wrong with them?" He had no idea. He'd never seen them act like this. Maybe Sheba had gone into heat early, or perhaps shared a home with a more aggressive dog and the others were picking up its scent on her. She began to whimper pathetically and he reached down to stroke her head.

The barking didn't stop, in fact it intensified, and he felt his anger begin to rise. This was all he needed. He was already later than he expected, and now the whole place was going nuts. *What am I going to do?* he asked himself. *I certainly can't cage up this poor dog with the others acting like . . . like a bunch of animals.*

"Quiet," he yelled.

They continued their frenzy. Some of the upper cages had actually begun to rock back and forth from the insane activity within.

Sheba was cowering by the door, desperate to leave. He didn't blame her in the least.

"Quiet," Aaron tried again, voice louder and full of authority.

The shepherd pup started to scratch at the door, digging deep gouges in the wood. He grabbed her by the collar to pull her away from it. The frightened dog began to urinate on the floor—the floor he had already mopped as one of his final duties of the evening.

Aaron's head began to throb with the insane baying; the odor of urine wafting through the air made his stomach roil. He couldn't stand it anymore.

"Quiet, or I'll have you all put to sleep!" he shrieked, his enraged voice reverberating off the walls of the white-tiled room.

The room went completely silent. Each and every dog suddenly calm, as if frightened by his words.

As if they had understood what he had said.

It was close to eleven by the time he finally stepped through the door of his home. Aaron removed his key from the lock and gently closed the front door behind him.

He stopped in the hallway, closed his eyes, and breathed in deeply, wallowing in the quiet. He could actually feel his body beginning to shut down.

The dogs had given him no further trouble after his emotional outburst. There wasn't so much as a whimper as he got Sheba settled in and mopped up her accident. They must have sensed that he meant business. Still, it was kind of strange, how they reacted. Then again, what did he expect after the kind of day he'd had.

Aaron trudged toward the kitchen. He was disappointed that Gabriel wasn't around to greet him, but figured the dog had probably gone up to bed when his foster parents put Stevie down for the night. The dog kept a very cautious eye on the autistic child, as if knowing he was special and needed to be looked after.

The light was on over the stove and a small piece of notepaper was held to the metal hood by a magnet in the shape of a cat's head. The note from his foster mother told him that everyone had gone to bed, and that his supper was in the oven. The note also mentioned a little surprise for him in the dining room. That made him smile.

Using a potholder, he removed the foil-wrapped plate from the oven and proceeded into the dining room. As he sat down he noticed a blue envelope leaning against a chocolate cupcake with a candle stuck in it. He picked up the card, wondering if he was supposed to light the candle and sing "Happy Birthday" to himself. He doubted he had the energy.

The card depicted a young man's dresser

covered in trophies for various sporting events, and said, "For a winning son." He opened the card and read something schmaltzy about the perfect boy growing into a man and rolled his eyes. Every year Lori bought the most sappy card she could find. He did the same for her birthday and Mother's Day. There was also a crisp new fifty-dollar bill stuck inside. Aaron sighed. He knew his foster parents couldn't afford this, but also knew it would be pointless to try to give it back. He'd tried before and they always insisted he keep it to buy himself something special.

He finished his dinner of meatloaf, mashed potatoes, and peas and was rinsing the dishes while mentally wrestling with the idea of what he was going to do next. Most of him just wanted to go to sleep, but the more studious part of him thought it best to at least attempt some homework.

Slowly he climbed the stairs to bed, leaning heavily on the rail, and popping the last of the cupcake into his mouth, his tired self busily shoving that academic part of his persona into a burlap sack. The door to Stevie's room at the top of the stairwell was ajar, and the light from a Barney nightlight streamed into the hall. He quietly stuck his head into the room to check on the child. Gabriel lay at the foot of the bed and began to wag his tail wildly when he saw Aaron. He crept carefully into the room and gave the dog's head a good rubbing.

Stevie moaned softly, deep in sleep, and Aaron pulled the covers up beneath his chin. He watched him for a moment, then gently touched the child's cheek before turning to leave.

At the door, he motioned with his head for Gabriel to follow. It was pretty much the same routine every evening. The dog would go to bed with Stevie, but once the child was asleep, he'd join Aaron for the night.

The big dog jumped down from the bed with a minimum of noise and headed down the hall. Watching Gabriel, Aaron fondly recalled when he had first seen the dog, tied up in a yard on Mal Street, his light yellow—almost white—coat of puppy fur covered with grease and mud. He was so tiny then, nothing like the moose he was today.

As he approached his own room, Aaron could hear the soft sounds of a television news broadcast coming from his parents' room across the hall. A timer would turn the television off at midnight. Talk about routine, Tom and Lori had been going to bed early and falling asleep in front of the news for as long as he could remember.

The door to his room was closed and he pushed it open, letting Gabriel in first. The dog hopped up onto the bed and stared at him with dark, vibrant eyes. His bright pink tongue lolled as he panted and his tail swung happily.

Aaron smiled as he closed the door. When he

first brought the dog home, he was so small that he couldn't even get onto the bed without help. Now he couldn't keep the beast off it. He often wondered what fate would have befallen the puppy if he hadn't stolen him from the Mal Street yard under the cover of darkness. Rumors were that the rundown tenement housed members of one of Lynn's street gangs, that they stole dogs and used them to train their pit bulls for fighting. With his first gaze into Gabriel's soulful eyes, Aaron knew there was no way he could ever let anything bad happen to the dog. The two had been inseparable since.

Aaron kicked off his sneakers and practically fell on the bed. Never had he felt anything more glorious. His lids, heavy with fatigue, gradually began to close, and he could already feel his body prepare for sleep.

The dog still stood over him, his heavy panting gently rocking the bed like one of those coin-operated, sleazy motel, magic-finger beds seen in movies.

"What's up, Gabe?" he asked, refusing to open his eyes.

The dog bounded from the bed in response and began to root around the room. Aaron moaned. He knew what that meant. The dog was looking for a toy.

He prayed to the god of dog toys that Gabriel's search would come up empty but the ancient deity of cheap rubber and squeakers seldom heard his pleas. The eighty-pound dog leaped back up on the bed. Even though his eyes were shut, Aaron knew that Gabriel loomed above him with something in his mouth.

"What do you want, Gabriel?" he asked groggily, knowing full well what the dog's response would be.

It was no surprise when he felt a tennis ball thump onto his chest.

What was a surprise was when the dog answered his question.

"Want to play ball now," Gabriel declared in a very clear and precise voice.

Aaron opened his eyes and gazed up into the grinning face of the animal. There was no doubt now. The day's descent into madness was complete. He was, in fact, losing his mind.

chapter three

Dr. Jonas seemed genuinely pleased to see him.

"You're not someone I'd expect to see waiting out front at eight thirty on a Friday morning, Aaron," the burly man said as he walked behind his desk, removed his tweed sports jacket, and hung it on a wooden coatrack stuck in the corner.

"How long has it been?" the psychiatrist asked, smiling warmly as he began to open the paper bag he'd carried in.

Aaron stood before the chair stationed in front of the doctor's desk. He glanced casually about the office. Little had changed since his last visit. Cream-colored walls, a framed Monet print bought in the gift shop of the Museum of Fine Arts—in a strange kind of way it felt comforting.

Dr. Michael Jonas had been his counselor after his placement with the Stanleys, and had done him a world of good. It was with his help that Aaron had learned to accept and cope with many of the curves life had seen fit to throw at him. The man had become a good friend and at the moment, Aaron was feeling a little guilty for not making more of an effort to keep in touch.

"I don't know, five years maybe?" he responded.

Jonas shook his shaggy head, smiling through his thick salt-and-pepper beard. "That long?" he mused as he removed a banana and a small bottle of orange juice from the bag. "Doesn't seem it, does it? But again, once you hit forty, the dinosaurs don't seem all that long ago." Jonas laughed at his own joke and sat down in the high-backed leather chair behind the sprawling oak desk. He grabbed the banana and juice and held them up to Aaron. "Do you want to share my breakfast? I'm sure I could find a fairly clean mug around here somewhere."

Aaron politely declined as he sat facing the doctor.

"Suit yourself," Jonas said. He twisted the metal cap off the juice and took a large gulp. "If you don't want breakfast, you must've skipped school for some other reason. What's going on, Aaron? What can I do for you?"

Aaron took in a deep breath and let it escape slowly, gathering his wits so as not to spew out the events of the past twenty-four hours in an incoherent babble. How exactly do you explain that you can suddenly understand foreign languages—and, oh yes, your dog has started to speak to you?

"You okay?" Jonas asked, starting to peel his banana. The man was smiling, but there was definitely a touch of concern in his tone.

Aaron shifted nervously in his seat. "I don't know," he answered with uncertainty.

"Why don't you tell me what's bothering you." Jonas broke off the top of the banana and popped the fruit into his waiting maw.

Aaron gripped the armrests tightly, sat back, and began to explain. "I'm not exactly sure what's happening . . . but I think I might be having some kind of breakdown."

The doctor took another swig of juice. "I doubt that very much," he said, "but if you want to explain, I'm all ears."

Aaron was very careful as he talked about what had happened at school the previous day, at the lockers with Vilma and her friends. He was sure to include that he had been experiencing a very bad headache just before he was suddenly able to understand their Portuguese. He decided to stop there, not yet wanting to broach the incident involving Gabriel.

Aaron had been staring at his sneakers through most of his explanation, and gradually looked up to meet Jonas's gaze as the psychiatrist finished the last of his banana.

"It's all right," Aaron said, again looking down at his feet. "If you want to call and get me a room up at Danvers State, I'll understand."

Jonas continued to chew as he picked up the fruit peel and threw it inside the empty paper bag. "This is interesting, Aaron," he said after swallowing. He wheeled his chair over to the side of his desk and tossed the bag into the trash barrel. "Very interesting."

"And I think . . . no, I know I could speak it if I had to," Aaron added, "and . . . and it's not just Portuguese." He thought of the conversations he'd had with his dog since last night. "Definitely not just Portuguese."

The doctor drank some more juice. "Let me get this straight," he said as he wiped the excess from his beard. "You had a headache and now you can understand and possibly speak foreign languages. A skill you've never had before. Is that what you're telling me?"

Aaron felt a flush of embarrassment bloom across his cheeks and leaned forward in his chair, studying his shoes. "I know it sounds really stupid but . . ."

"It doesn't sound stupid," Dr. Jonas said, *"but it does sound a little weird. Do you have any other symptoms?"*

Aaron looked up. "No. Do you think it has anything to do with my headache?"

The doctor had been smiling, but his smile gradually began to fade as Aaron spoke.

"Is . . . is there something wrong?" he asked.

Jonas reached over to a pile of papers at the corner of his desk and removed a yellow legal pad. "You understood what I just said to you?" he asked, picking up a pen and writing something on the pad.

Aaron nodded. "Sure, why?"

"What exactly did I say?"

Aaron thought for a minute. "You said that what I was saying wasn't stupid, although it was weird and did I have any other symptoms."

Jonas stroked his beard. "I was speaking to you in Spanish, Aaron."

Aaron squirmed nervously in his chair. "But . . . but I don't know Spanish."

"You've never taken it in school?" Jonas asked. "Or had friends who spoke it?"

Aaron shook his head. "The only language I ever took in school was French, and I never got a grade higher than a C."

Jonas nodded and began to write again. Finished, he set his pen down on the pad and looked up. "Describe your headache to me, Aaron—but do it in Spanish."

Aaron rubbed at his temple. "In Spanish?" He smiled uneasily. "All right, here goes." Aaron opened his mouth and began to speak. *"It was like somebody was sticking a knife into my head."* He touched the top of his head. *"Right here. Like somebody put it through my skull into my brain. I've never had a headache like it, I can tell you that."*

He stopped, and a lopsided grin crept across his features. "How was that?" he asked, returning to English.

The doctor was shaking his head in disbelief. "Impressive," he said, failing to keep his growing interest in check.

Aaron leaned forward, eager to know why this was happening to him. "So you don't think I'm crazy or anything? You believe me, Doc?"

The desk chair creaked in protest as the doctor leaned back. He held the pen in one hand and was tapping it against the palm of the other. "I believe you. I just don't know what to make of it," he said thoughtfully. "Let's see. . . . "

Aaron watched as the big man wheeled his chair over to a bookcase against the wall on the other side of his desk. He disappeared as he bent down to take something from the bottom shelf. When he came up, he laid a large text on top of the desk. Aaron could not see what its subject was, and waited nervously as the doctor thumbed through the pages.

"If you . . . can tell me . . . what I'm saying to you . . . right now," he said, struggling with the complexity of the words he pulled from the book, *"I'll have no choice . . . but . . . to believe . . . the incredible."* Jonas looked up from the text and stared with eager eyes.

"I understood you perfectly," Aaron said. "It was Latin, right?"

The doctor slowly nodded, looking stunned.

"It looks as though we're both going to have to start to believe in the incredible," Aaron said.

Jonas's expression was that of a man who had just been witness to a miracle. His eyes bulged as he slowly closed the Latin text. "Aaron, I . . . I don't know what to say."

Aaron was growing a bit nervous. The doctor was staring at him, and he felt like a bug beneath a microscope. "Why do you think it happened?" he asked, to break the sudden silence. "How? . . ."

Jonas was shaking his head again as he combed his large fingers through his graying beard. "I have no idea, but the fact that you had such a powerful headache before this talent manifested suggests that the *how* is likely neurological."

"Neurological?" Aaron questioned, suddenly concerned. "Like there's something wrong with my brain—like a tumor or something?"

The psychiatrist leaned forward in his chair again. "Not necessarily," he said, stressing the words with his large hands. "I've heard stories of neurological disorders that caused individuals to gain unique abilities."

"Like understanding and speaking foreign languages?" Aaron suggested.

Jonas nodded. "Exactly. The case I'm thinking of involved a man from Michigan, I believe. After suffering severe head trauma in a skating accident, he found himself able to calculate the most complex math problems in his head. He hadn't even finished high school, never mind classes in mathematical theory."

"So you think that something like that might have happened to me?" Aaron asked the psychiatrist.

The doctor pondered the possibility. "Maybe something happened inside your brain that's caused this unique capability to develop."

Jonas grabbed his pen again and furiously began to take notes. "I have a friend over at Mass General, a neurologist. We could talk to him—after we've done some testing of our own of course and—"

The sudden rapping at the office door made Aaron jump.

The doctor pulled up his sleeve and glanced at his watch. "Damn it," he said with a hiss. "My nine thirty must be here."

Aaron's heart still pounded in his chest from the sudden scare. He watched Dr. Jonas step out from behind his desk and move toward the door.

"Excuse me for a moment, Aaron," he said as he opened the door and stepped into the lobby.

Alone, Aaron's mind began to race. *What if there is something wrong with me—something wrong with my brain?* He began to bite at his thumbnail. Maybe it would be wise to make an appointment with the family physician just in case.

He thought about missing another day of school and felt himself begin to panic. This business couldn't be coming at a worse time. He'd be hearing from colleges shortly and needed his grades to reflect how serious he was about getting into the schools of his choice. He wondered if colleges looked at the number of absences before making their acceptance decisions.

The door opened. "Sorry about that, kid," he said, moving behind his desk. "Listen, I'm booked solid for the entire day, but why don't you come by tomorrow and see me. How would that be?"

Aaron stood. "It's Saturday. Is that all right?"

Jonas nodded. "Sure, I was going to be in tomorrow anyway. Why don't you stop by—say early afternoon? We can do a few more tests before I give my buddy at Mass General a ring."

Aaron agreed with a slight nod and walked to the door. "Thanks for seeing me this morning, Doc," he said, a hand on the doorknob. "I'm sorry it's been so long."

Dr. Jonas was removing a file from inside a cabinet beside his desk. "No problem, Aaron," he said as he opened the file. "It was good to see you."

Aaron had opened the door and was about to leave when Jonas spoke again to him, bringing him back into the office. The man was standing, looking calm and confident.

"Relax," the psychiatrist said. "We'll work

this out, I promise. See you tomorrow."

As he stepped out into the morning sunshine, Aaron could not shake the gnawing feeling that something was suddenly not right with his world.

Something over which he had no control.

Aaron crossed the street and stepped over the low, dark green, pipe fence that encircled Lynn Common.

He'd arrived early to his former psychiatrist's office, so he had parked on the other side of the common and waited there. He'd always enjoyed this place, with its oak trees and unkept grass. Even though it was a bit rundown, it still had its charms. Besides the beach, it was one of his favorite places to walk Gabriel when the fickle New England weather cooperated.

He walked across the expanse of green trying to clear his head. As he reached the middle of the open area, he remembered an odd bit of Lynn trivia: the common had been built in the shape of a shoe. The voice of his junior high history teacher, Mr. Frost, droned on in his brain about the history of the city.

Settled in 1629, Lynn ultimately became a major producer of shoes. Though the construction of the common was first begun in 1630, the present-day sections were shaped into the approximate proportions of a shoe during the nineteenth century, the larger area being the sole, and the smaller, the heel. At that moment, Aaron was inside the sole.

He'd always wanted to take a helicopter ride over the city to verify that the common was indeed in the shape of a shoe. Mr. Frost had talked about a book at the library that contained an aerial shot of the common. Since he had planned to finish out the day at the library anyway, perhaps he'd take the time to look it up, he thought as he continued on a path to his car.

Aaron suddenly shuddered, as if someone had just slipped an ice cube along his spine. The strange feeling that he was being watched rolled over him in waves, and he stopped to look around.

He glanced at the ancient bandstand squatting in the center of the sole. The shabby structure was once used for summer band concerts, but was now more of a hangout for kids skipping school or people passing time between unemployment checks. Today it was empty.

He continued to look about, and there, just where the heel began, he could make out a figure standing over one of the "Keep Lynn Beautiful" trash barrels. There was a shopping cart parked near the man. *Probably collecting cans for the deposit money,* Aaron thought as he continued on his way, studying the lone figure in the distance. Yes, he was sure of it. The man was staring at him. Aaron could actually feel his gaze upon him.

"Probably deciding whether he should run over and hit me up for change," he muttered beneath his breath as he reached the other side of the common.

Aaron stepped over the low fence. His metallic blue, '95 Toyota Corolla was parked directly across the street, and he waited for an opportunity to cross. As he fished his keys from his pocket he thought about what he would do for the rest of the day. He had skipped school, but it didn't mean that he was going to shirk all his academic responsibilities. He'd spend the afternoon in the library beginning his research for Ms. Mulholland's senior English paper, a paper required for graduation. He hoped a look around the library would help him decide on a topic. Ideas danced around in his head: the duality of good and evil in the works of Edgar Allan Poe, Herman Melville and religious symbolism, Shakespeare's use of—

The hair at the back of his neck suddenly stood on end. His senses screamed. Someone was behind him.

Aaron whirled around and came face to face with the man he'd seen at the barrel far across the common. The old man was dressed in a filthy overcoat, pants worn at the knees, and sneakers. The faint smell of body odor and alcohol wafted off him, and Aaron almost gagged on the unpleasant stench.

He was taken aback, not sure of what to do

as the man began to lean toward him. *What the hell is he doing?*

The man appeared to be smelling him. He moved in close to Aaron and sniffed at his face, his hair, his chest, and then he stepped back. He nodded, as if in response to a question to which only he was privy.

"Can . . . can I help you with something?" Aaron stammered.

The man responded, speaking in a language Aaron had never heard before, a language he somehow sensed had not been uttered by anyone in a very long time.

"Can you understand the tongue of the messenger, boy?" asked the old man in the arcane dialect.

Aaron answered in kind. *"Yes,"* he said, the strange words feeling incredibly odd as they rolled off his tongue. *"I can understand you . . . but I don't understand the question."*

The old man continued to stare, his gaze even more intense. Aaron could have sworn that he saw what appeared to be a single flame dancing in the center of each ancient eye, but knew that it was probably just a trick of the light.

"You answer my question as you speak," the man responded, still using the bizarre-sounding language, *"and what you are becomes obvious to me."*

"What . . . what I am?" Aaron asked. *"I don't understand what . . ."*

The strange old man shuffled closer. *"Nephilim,"* he whispered as he raised a dirty hand to point. *"You are Nephilim."*

The word reverberated through Aaron's skull and a sudden panic gripped him. He had to get away. He had to get away from this strange old man, from that word. He had to get away as fast as he could.

"I really have to be going," he muttered as he slipped his key into the lock and hauled open the car door.

Aaron got inside his car and locked it. He couldn't remember a time when the need to run was so strong. He put the key into the ignition and turned the engine over. As he put the car in drive, he chanced a look at the old man. He was still standing there, staring in at him with those intense eyes.

Aaron turned away and pulled out into traffic. He glanced in the rearview mirror at the old man receding in the distance. He continued to stand there, watching him drive away, mouth moving, repeating a single word. Aaron knew what he was saying.

The old man was saying "Nephilim," over and over again.

Nephilim.

Aaron splashed cold water on his face and stared at his dripping features in the water-speckled mirror of the Lynn Public Library's restroom.

What the hell is going on? he thought, studying his reflection. *What's happening to me?*

There was fear in the face that looked back from the mirror. *What was that with the old man?* he wondered for the thousandth time. *What did he mean by the language of messengers—and what's a Nephilim?* His thoughts raced feverishly.

He pulled some paper towels from the dispenser on the wall and wiped the water from his face. As he reached to the side of the sink for the restroom key, attached to an unusually large piece of wood, he noticed that his hand was shaking. Aaron snatched up the key and clenched the wood tightly in his grasp.

"Gotta calm down," he told himself in a whisper. "The old guy was just crazy, probably done the exact same routine to ten other people today. What are you getting so worked up over? You know this city is loaded with kooks."

There was a gentle knock at the bathroom door. He took a deep breath, composed himself, and opened the door. An old man was standing there with a coat slung over his arm.

"You done in there?" he asked with a nervous smile.

Aaron did the best that he could to return the pleasantries as he stepped out of the restroom. "Yeah, sorry I took so long," he said as he handed the old-timer the block of wood with the key attached.

"No problem," the old man said as he took

the key and moved into the bathroom. "Just wanted to make sure you didn't fall in."

Aaron turned as the door closed and saw that the man was chuckling. He didn't much feel like it, but found himself laughing at the man's good-natured dig anyway. "Wouldn't that have been the icing on the cake if I had," he said to himself as he climbed the white marble steps from the basement to the first floor.

He found an empty table far in the corner of one of the reading rooms and slung his jacket over the back of a chair. He wasn't sure how much he'd be able to accomplish now, but at least he had to make an attempt. Besides, he needed something to distract him from the bizarreness that seemed to be following him of late. He had brought a notebook in with him and removed a pen from its front pocket.

He settled in and spent hours perusing books on a number of different authors and literary subjects, searching for something that piqued his interest enough for a research paper. He'd pretty much made up his mind to go with the topic of good and evil's duality in the works of Poe, when he realized that he had zoned out, and had been doodling in the border of his notepad, writing something over and over with a variety of spellings.

Nefellum. Nefilem. Nifillim. Nephilem. Nephilim.

Aaron tore out the page and stared at it. *What does it mean? Why can't I just forget about it?*

he wondered, reviewing each of the spellings.

He got up from his chair and headed into the reference area of the library. The first book that he pulled from the shelves was a *Webster's New World College Dictionary.* He placed the large book down onto a table and began to look for the word, trying all the incarnations he had written. He found nothing.

Maybe it doesn't mean a thing, he thought as he returned the dictionary to where he had found it. *Maybe it's just a nonsense word made up by a crazy person, and I'm equally nuts for giving it this much attention.*

Aaron decided that he had already wasted enough time and energy on the old man's rants, and headed back to his table to begin an outline for his paper. If anything could be salvaged from this train wreck of a day, at least he could get a head start on that.

He crumpled up the piece of paper in his hand and headed back to the reading room.

But the word continued to jump around in his head, as if it had a life of its own and was taunting him. Nephilim.

Aaron casually glanced into the library's computer room as he passed. The usually crowded room was surprisingly empty, with several stations free.

Seizing the opportunity to satisfy his curiosity, he walked in and sat down at one of the computers. This would be it, the mystery word's last chance to mean something. If he didn't find it here, he would purge it from his mind forever and never think of it again. He signed in with a password that he had obtained from the library his first year of high school, and called up a search engine that he used often when researching information for school papers. The screen appeared and, choosing one of the varied spellings, he typed in the mystery word. He hit the Enter key and held his breath. The page cleared and then some information appeared.

"Do you mean Nephilim?" asked the message that appeared on top of the new page.

He maneuvered the mouse and brought the arrow over to the revised spelling, clicked once and waited as the new pages loaded.

Aaron was startled to see how many sites appeared with some kind of connection to the word. *So much for it being nonsense,* he thought as he scrolled down the page, reading a bit about each of the sites. There were multiple sites about a rock group, some about a role-playing game, all using the name Nephilim, but none gave a meaning.

A site that specialized in religious mythologies finally caught his attention. *Is that it?* he wondered, as the page began to upload. *Does it have something to do with religion?* In that case, it was no wonder he had no familiarity with it. He'd never been much of a religious person, and neither had the Stanleys.

The site appeared to be a who's who of people, places, and things from the Bible, and the first thing he saw was a definition that he eagerly read.

> The biblical term *Nephilim,* which in Hebrew means "the fallen ones" or "those who fell," refers to the offspring of angels and mortal women mentioned in Genesis 6: 1–4. A fuller account is preserved in the apocryphal Book of Enoch, which recounts how a group of angels left heaven to mate with women, and taught humanity such heinous skills as the art of war.

Aaron sat back in his chair, stunned. *Offspring of angels and mortal women,* he read again. "What the hell does that have to do with me?" he muttered, moving closer to the computer screen.

Somebody coughed behind him, and he turned to see four people waiting in the doorway of the computer room. A heavyset kid with a bad case of acne, wearing an *X-Men* T-shirt, tapped the face of his Timex watch and glared at him.

Aaron looked back to the screen and quickly read a bit more before closing the site and signing out. He removed his pen from his pocket and on the wrinkled piece of paper where he had written his various attempts at the mystery word, he crossed out the incorrect spellings leaving only the correct one.

Nephilim.

Sighing heavily, he returned to his seat and his books in the other room. He sat down with every intention of working on his paper, but found that he could not concentrate, his thoughts stalled on the story of human women having babies with angels. A shiver of unease ran up and down his spine as he chillingly recalled the subject of his recurring dream. Again he saw the boy attacked by the winged creatures dressed in golden armor. It was too much of a coincidence to ignore.

He got to his feet and snatched up the notepad from the table. He had to find out more. It was as if something was compelling him to dig deeper. *Maybe there's some way I can maneuver this into a research subject*, he mused.

Aaron used another computer in the lobby of the building to search the library's inventory, and found that most of what he was looking for was kept in a separate room off the reference area.

He wrote the titles down on his notepad and began his search. In a book called *The Lost Books of Eden*, Aaron learned more about the Book of Enoch. It was an apochryphal book of the Old Testament, written in Hebrew about a century before the birth of Christ. The original version was lost near the end of the fourth century, and only fragments remained until Bruce the Traveler brought back a copy from Abyssinia in 1773, probably made from a version known to the early Greek fathers.

What followed were some passages from the ancient text of Enoch, and what Aaron read summed up all that he had learned so far:

> . . . that there were angels who consented to fall from heaven that they might have intercourse with the daughters of the earth. For in those days the sons of men having multiplied, there were born to them daughters of great beauty. And when the angels, or sons of heaven, beheld them, they were filled with desire; wherefore they said to one another: "Come let us choose wives from among the race of man, and let us beget children."

Aaron was amazed. He'd never heard of such a thing. His knowledge of angels was limited to what was often found on holiday cards or at the tops of Christmas trees—beautiful women in flowing, white gowns, or children with tiny wings, and halos perched on their heads.

Fascinated, he was reaching for the list of books he'd yet to examine when again he was overcome with the feeling of being observed. He quickly turned in his chair, half expecting to see the crazy old man pointing his gnarly finger and calling him Nephilim over and over again—but was shocked to see Vilma Santiago.

The girl gave him the sweetest of smiles and meekly came into the room. "I thought that was you," she said with only the slightest hint of an accent.

"Yep, it's me," he said nervously as he stood up from his chair. *"I'm just doing some, y'know, research and stuff for Ms. Mulholland's research paper and . . ."*

Vilma looked at him strangely and he stopped talking, afraid that his nose had started to run, or something equally gross and embarrassing had happened.

"Is . . . is something wrong?" he asked, tempted to reach up and quickly rub his nose.

The girl shook her head and grinned from ear to ear. "No, nothing is wrong," she said happily. "I just didn't know that you could speak Portuguese."

He was confused at first, wondering how she could have known about his sudden power, when he realized what he had done.

"Was I . . . was I just speaking to you in Portuguese?"

She giggled and covered her mouth with a delicate hand. "Yes, yes, you were, and quite well, I might add. Where did you learn it?"

He had no idea how to answer. Aaron

shrugged his shoulders. "Just picked it up, I guess. I'm pretty good with languages."

Vilma nodded. "Yes, you are."

There was a moment of uncomfortable silence, and then she looked down at the table and the books he was reading.

"That's just some stuff I'm looking through to get ideas. I haven't decided yet, but I might . . ."

She picked up a book called *Angels: From A to Z* and began to thumb through it. "I love this one," she said as she flipped the pages. "Everything you could want to know about angels and even a section at the back of the book that lists movies about angels." She looked up from the open book in her hands and squinted her eyes in deep thought. "I really think this one might be my favorite."

Vilma placed the book back onto the table and began to rummage through the other volumes. "I love anything to do with angels." She reached into her shirt and removed something delicate on the end of a gold chain. "Look at this."

Aaron looked closer to see that it was an angel. "That's really pretty," he said, looking from the golden angel to her. At the moment, the necklace wasn't the only thing he found pretty.

"Thanks," she said, putting the jewelry back inside her shirt. "I just love them, they make me feel safe—y'know?"

Aaron could have been knocked over with a

feather—angel or otherwise. He just stood there and smiled as he watched the girl go through the books he had pulled from the shelves. It must have been some weird form of synchronicity, he imagined. *What are the odds?* It boggled his already addled brain.

"Is this what you are planning to do your paper on?" Vilma asked excitedly, interrupting his thoughts.

"I don't know . . . yeah, maybe," he stammered, unsure of his answer. "Yeah, maybe I will. Seems like it might be really interesting."

She beamed as she began to talk about the topic. "It's fascinating. When I was little and lived in Brazil, my auntie would tell me stories of how the angels would visit the villages in the jungles disguised as travelers and . . ."

Vilma suddenly stopped her story and looked away from him. "I'm sorry for babbling, it's just that I find it so very interesting, and to get a chance to talk about it with somebody else, well, I really enjoy it is all."

She seemed embarrassed, going suddenly quiet as she pulled at the sleeves of her denim jacket.

"It's all right, really," Aaron said with a smile that he hoped wasn't too goofy. He snatched his notepad off the table. "Maybe, if you're not too busy, you could help me with my research."

Her eyes grew wide in excitement.

"The stories from Brazil, the ones your aunt

told you? They would probably be really cool to talk about in the paper, if you didn't mind helping me."

He couldn't believe what he was doing. Vilma Santiago, the hottest girl in the Lynn public schools, and he was asking her to help him with his research paper. *What an absolute idiot,* he berated himself.

"That would be really fun," she said, nodding her head in agreement. "I even have some other books you could use."

Aaron was in complete and utter shock. The girl of his dreams had agreed to help him with his paper, and actually seemed to be excited about doing it. He had no idea what to say next, afraid that if he opened his mouth to speak, something completely stupid would spill out and he'd ruin everything.

Vilma was silent also, nervously looking at the books on the table then back to him. She glanced at her watch.

"Well, I have to catch the bus," the girl said, walking toward the doorway. "Maybe we can talk some more about your paper in school Monday—you *will* be in school Monday, won't you?" She smirked.

He couldn't believe it. She actually noticed that he was absent today. Maybe there was something to what she had said to her friends yesterday. Maybe she actually did think he was cute.

"I'll be there," he said. "All day in fact."

She laughed and gave him a small wave as she stepped out of the room. "I'll see you Monday, Aaron. Have a good weekend."

He could do nothing but stand there, numbed with disbelief. It was almost enough to make him forget all about the disturbing dreams, his strange new linguistic skills, and the cryptic ramblings of a crazy old man.

Almost.

chapter four

Samuel Chia lay upon his bed, twisted in sheets of the finest silk, and dreamed of flying. Of all that was lost to him, he missed that the most.

It was not true sleep by human standards, but it was a way for him to remember a time precious to him, the time before his fall.

Sam rolled onto his back and opened his eyes to the new day. He did not need to check a clock to tell him the hour; he knew it to be precisely eight A.M., for that was when he wished to rise.

He lay quietly and listened to the sounds of Hong Kong outside and far below his penthouse apartment. If he so wished, he could listen in on the conversations of the city's inhabitants as they lived out their drastically short existences. But today he had little interest.

Sam rose from his bed and padded naked across the mahogany floor to stand in front of the enormous floor-to-ceiling windows that looked out over the city. A Chinese junk, its sails unfurled, caught his attention as it cruised gracefully across the emerald green water of Victoria Bay. He had lived in many places in his long life on this planet, but none brought him as much solace as this place. China spoke to him. It told him that everything would be all right, and on most days, he believed that to be true.

He pressed his forehead against the thick glass and allowed himself to feel the cold of its surface. His naked skin responded with prickled gooseflesh, and although he reveled in the human experience, everyday he longed for what he once had, for what was lost when he refused to take a side in the Great War.

His head still pressed against the window, Sam opened his eyes and gazed at the panorama before him.

Yes, he longed for the glory that was once his, but each day this place—this wondrous sight sought to seduce him with its vitality. A distraction that sometimes made it easier to accept his fate.

Sometimes.

Sam was slipping into his black silk robe, enjoying the sensation upon his pale, sculpted flesh, when the phone began to chirp.

He knew who was calling. Not from any innate psychic ability, but because she called each morning at this very time.

Joyce Woo was the human woman he allowed to manage his various business affairs, including his nightclubs, casinos, and restaurants.

Sam strolled from the bedroom to the chrome-and-tile kitchen and let the machine pick up. He decided to play a little game—to see if he could guess the problems she was calling to report. What trivial piece of nonsense would she choose to annoy him with this time? he wondered: an unexpected shortage of truffles at his French restaurant perhaps, or the local constabulary requiring increased compensation for their lack of interest in certain illicit activities performed at his clubs, or maybe she was finally calling to confess that she'd been skimming off the top of his earnings for the last nine months.

Sam popped a cork on a bottle of Dom Perignon and drank from it as he listened to the message.

"Good morning, Mr. Chia. This is Joyce," said a woman's voice in Cantonese.

He toasted the incoming call with the bottle.

"There was an incident at the Pearl Club last night that may require you to speak with the chief of police. I can give you more details when you come into the office this morning, but I wanted you to be aware."

He could hear her turn the page of a pad of paper where she had written her notes.

"And be reminded that you have a two

o'clock conference with the zoning committee about the Pier Road project."

Believing that she had finished, he walked through the kitchen, bottle in hand, toward the bathroom. But she began to speak again. He paused in the hall to listen.

"Oh yes," she said, "an old friend of yours—a Mr. Verchiel, stopped by the office this morning. He said he will only be in town for a short time and hoped the two of you could get together."

"Verchiel," he whispered. The bottle dropped from his hand to the floor, shattering and spilling the expensive contents onto the black and white tiles.

"He said that he will be in touch," Joyce said from the machine. "There are a few other items, but we can discuss them when you get here. Good morning, sir."

The line disconnected and still he didn't move.

Verchiel.

Sam Chia bounded to his bedroom and threw open the doors of the heavy wooden armoire. He shed his robe and pulled out clothes. There would be no time for a shower today and he would not be going into the office.

He had to leave Hong Kong. It was as simple as that. If Verchiel had found him, then there was no doubt that the Powers had come to China. And if that were the case, then none of his ilk was safe.

Sam finished buttoning his white cotton shirt

and began to tuck its tails inside his pants. He cinched the brown leather belt around his waist.

He thought briefly about contacting the others, to warn them of the Powers' presence, but decided against it for it was likely already too late.

He slipped his bare, delicate feet into a pair of Italian loafers and donned a navy blue sports jacket.

He would go to Europe; France would suffice. He would stay in Paris until Verchiel and his dogs left China. Joyce could manage his affairs until he returned.

Sam placed his billfold inside his coat pocket and picked up the phone to summon his driver. He would go to the airport, charter a plane, and contact Joyce once in flight.

"Are you going out, Samchia?" asked a voice from somewhere in the room.

Startled, Sam dropped the phone and spun around to face the voice.

"How disappointing," said the man in the gray trench coat standing in the living room in front of the sixty-inch digital television. "After we've spent all this time searching for you."

There was a small, dirty child with him who pressed its unwashed face against the smoothness of the television screen and licked eagerly at his reflection.

"I'm sorry, do you prefer being called by your monkey name—Samuel Chia?" Verchiel asked as he slid his hands inside his coat pockets and began to slowly advance toward him. The child followed, heeling obediently at his side.

"What do you want?" Sam asked as the man approached.

Verchiel's dark eyes roamed about the luxurious living quarters taking in every extravagant detail.

"Did you think that these would hide you from me?" he asked, pointing to a series of arcane symbols painted on the penthouse walls. To the human eye they appeared as decoration, but in actuality, they were much more than that.

The feral child had hopped up onto Sam's leather coach, jumping from foot to foot, as he muttered happily to himself in a singsong voice.

"The spell of concealment must have gone stale with all the recent changes here," Verchiel said, making reference to the recent shift in Chinese government. "My hound caught scent of you as soon as we arrived." He patted the child's head affectionately as he passed the sofa. "You live like a king amongst the animals," the pale-skinned man said as he fixed his bottomless black gaze upon Sam. "For this you abandoned Paradise?"

Verchiel's words stung like the barbed end of a whip's lash.

"You know that's untrue, Verchiel. I left because I did not want to choose sides. I loved the Morningstar, as I loved all my brethren, but to question the Almighty—I could think of no other solution but to flee." Sam lowered his head, disgraced by his admission. Even after all this time, his actions shamed him.

"A coward by your own admission," Verchiel said with a snarl as he moved closer. "If only the others could be so honest."

The phone began to ring again, and Sam watched Verchiel's attention turn to the device as the recorded message played out and Joyce began to speak.

"Joyce again, sir. Mr. Dalton from the licensing board just called and asked if you could reschedule Monday's meeting to—"

A blast of searing white light erupted from Verchiel's hand and melted the phone into nothing more than sputtering, black plastic slag. Startled, the child leaped from the sofa and ran to hide, as if sensing the violence that was sure to follow.

"The sound of their voices," Verchiel said, his right hand gesturing toward his ear, "like the chattering of animals. It annoys me to no end." Verchiel glided closer. "How do you stand it?"

Sam clenched his fists. Anger unlike any he had ever experienced coursed through his body. Perhaps he *had* spent too much time among the humans, he thought. Their rabid emotions had obviously begun to rub off on him.

"I'll ask you again, why have you come here?"

Verchiel cocked his head to one side. "Is it

not obvious, brother?" he asked. "Have you not been awaiting me since your fall?"

"Yes," he hissed, "but it's been years—thousands of years."

Verchiel shook his head as he replied. "A second, an hour, a millenium; increments of time that mean nothing to the Powers," he said with a cold indifference. "You have sinned against the Allfather, and time does not change that fact."

Sam began to back away. "Haven't I suffered enough?" he asked. "My self-imposed exile on this world has taught me that—"

Verchiel's hand shot up into the air in a gesture to silence him. "Cease your mewling; I do not wish to hear it." The leader of the Powers pointed toward the windows behind him. "You sound like one of them." There was revulsion in his voice.

Sam knew it was probably for naught, but if there was anything he learned from living among humans, it was that it didn't hurt to try. "But isn't it enough that I have been denied the voice of my Father, that my true aspect is but a shadow of my former glory? Does this not count for anything?" He touched his chest as he continued his plea. "You may not believe it, but I have suffered."

Verchiel again looked about the opulent living space. A cruel grin began to form on his pale white features as he fixed Sam with his icy stare.

"Suffered, have you?" he asked as he began

to spread his arms. "Your suffering hasn't even begun."

Sam experienced a strange sense of elation mixed with sheer terror as he watched the enormous wings erupt from Verchiel's back.

I once had wings as mighty, he remembered with overwhelming sadness. Wings that could have taken him away from this place, allowed him to flee the judgment of Verchiel. But that was long, long ago, and what were once mighty, were now nothing more than an atrophied shadow of their former glory.

Verchiel began to rhythmically move his wings and the penthouse was suddenly filled with winds as strong as tropical storms.

"Verchiel, please," Sam pleaded, just before a crystal ashtray hit him in the face. It opened a bleeding gash above his right eye.

Sam's body went limp and he ceased to struggle against the currents for a brief moment. He was picked up by the powerful gale and hurled backward, pinned against the picture windows. As he slammed against the glass, the sound of something cracking filled his ears, and he wondered if it was the window behind him or his bones.

Verchiel's wings beat the air with ferocious abandon, their furious movement a ghostly blur.

"There is no mercy for what you have done, Samchia!" Verchiel shrieked over the pounding of the air. "Your time has come, as it will come for all the others who have fallen from His grace!"

Sam tried to pull himself away from the window, but the strength of the wind was too great. He wanted to speak, to scream out that he was truly sorry for his sins, but the blood from his head wound streamed down his face into his mouth, silencing him. He had never even seen his own blood, but now it was filling his mouth with its foul taste.

The inch-thick pane of window glass behind him began to crack and spiderweb across its surface. Windows that had been built to withstand powerful storms from the Pacific Ocean were no match for the power of Verchiel.

Again Sam struggled to speak. "Verchiel . . . ," he managed to bellow above the sounds of his brother's merciless wings.

Verchiel continued his advance, wings flapping faster and faster still. "I can't hear you!" he screamed in response.

Sam yelled all the louder. "Tell Him—tell Him that I'm sorry." He could see the look of revulsion on Verchiel's face, and knew his words of repentance were heard.

A heavy chrome kitchen chair tumbled away from the table, and as if made of tin, was propelled through the air toward him.

Sam closed his eyes on the horrible visage of Verchiel, his wings unmercifully assaulting the air. His time was at an end, of this he was certain. What he had feared most since falling to Earth was finally to claim him.

Samuel Chia, formerly Samchia of the Heavenly Host, willed his mind elsewhere, to a time before the war, before impossible choices, before the fall.

The chrome projectile did not strike him directly, but smashed into the window to the left of him, shattering the glass, allowing it to give way beneath the turbulent force of Verchiel's wings.

Within a twinkling shower of razor-sharp glass and debris, Sam fell yet again.

And as he descended to his end, he dreamed.

He dreamed of flying.

Gabriel trotted happily into the living room where the Stanleys had assembled for Chinese takeout and the weekly Friday night movie rental. He was proudly holding a purple stuffed toy in his mouth.

Aaron sat on the floor with Stevie building a multicolored tower with Duplo blocks. Occasionally he looked up at the television to see what Mr. Schwarzenegger was blowing up. The fact that this was at least the third time his foster dad had rented the movie in the last six months didn't bother him. The night was all about distraction, anything to keep from thinking about the strange incidents of the last two days. Except for the conversation with Vilma Santiago, he wished he could forget them completely.

The dog dropped the purple toy before Aaron and it rolled to topple the Duplo tower.

"Gabriel," Aaron said, annoyed, as he batted the toy aside and attempted to right the structure.

"Play with Goofy Grape now," Gabriel demanded with a wag of his thick, muscular tail.

Aaron ignored him and helped the child select some more blocks to fortify the tower.

Gabriel lunged forward and snatched up the toy with his mouth. He gave it a ferocious shake and let it fly. The stuffed toy bounced off young Stevie's head and landed among the piles of unused blocks.

"Goofy Grape now," the dog said even louder.

Aaron glared at the animal. "No Goofy Grape," he said sternly, referring to the toy that he had nicknamed because it resembled an enormous grape with a face. "I'm playing with Stevie now. Go lie down."

He could feel the dog's intense stare upon him, as if he were attempting to use mind powers to sway his decision. Aaron didn't bother to look up, hoping the dog would eventually grow tired and go away.

Gabriel abruptly turned and quickly strolled from the room.

Good, Aaron thought, connecting a blue block to a yellow. He didn't want to hear the dog talking tonight. To anyone else it was typical dog noise, a series of whines, growls, and barks, but to Aaron it was a language—a language he could easily understand. Tonight he wanted it to be like it used to be. A bark, an excited wag of the tail—that was all the conversation he really needed from his four-legged friend.

From the couch Tommy Stanley let out a happy guffaw in response to one of the movie hero's patented catch phrases.

"No one says 'em like Arnold," his foster father said aloud, a critical observation about the art of action films. "Your Van Dammes, Seagals—they're all well and good with the fightin' and blowin' up crap, but nobody delivers the goods like *Ahnold.*" He said the name with a mock Austrian accent and then went back to watching the film, sucked into the cinematic world of a one-man army out to rescue his little girl from the bad guys.

Aaron heard the sound of toenails clicking across the kitchen linoleum toward the living room, and then a strange grunting sound. He didn't even have to see what the dog was bringing from his toy box; he knew just from the sound. Squeaky Pig was on its way.

Gabriel came around the corner, a pink stuffed pig clutched in his maw. With his muscular jaws he squeezed the body of the pig repeatedly, and it emitted a sound very much like that of a pig grunting.

As before, the dog approached and let the toy fall to the floor.

"Squeaky Pig better," he said with a hint of

excitement in his gruff-sounding language. *"Play with Squeaky Pig."*

Aaron felt his temper rising. He was angry with the day and all the stuff that had happened, angry with the dog for reminding him that things are not how they used to be, angry with himself for being angry.

"He's pretty vocal tonight," Lori said from the recliner, looking up from her book. When she had seen what movie her husband brought back from the video store, she had gone upstairs to get out her latest romance novel. "Does he need to go out or something?"

The dog is being "vocal," he thought. *If you only knew the half of it.*

"No," he said, giving Gabriel the evil eye. "He doesn't need to go out, he's just being a pain in the butt."

Gabriel flinched as if he'd been struck. He blinked his soulful, brown eyes repeatedly and lowered his ears flat against his skull.

"Not pain in the butt," the dog grumbled as he began to back from the room, his tail lowered and partially stuck between his legs. *"Just wanted to play with Aaron. Bad dog. Go lie down. Bad dog."*

He turned and sadly slunk from the room.

Gabriel's words stung. *How could I be so cruel?* Aaron thought disgustedly. Here he was with the unique ability to understand exactly what the dog wanted—to be played with, to be shown some attention—and he was so caught up in his own problems that he couldn't be bothered to give in to the dog's simple request. *I ought'a be ashamed.*

"Gabriel," he called out. Aaron had to call for him two more times before the dog finally responded, peeking around the doorframe.

"C'mere," he said, patting the floor with his hand and smiling. "Come over here."

Gabriel bounded into the room tail wagging, and began to lick Aaron's face excitedly.

"Gabriel not pain in butt, yes?" he asked between licks.

"No," Aaron answered, taking the dog's blockhead in his two hands and looking directly into his brown eyes. "You're not a pain in the butt; you're a good boy."

"I'm a good boy," the dog happily repeated, and began to lick his face again.

Gabriel plopped his large body down beside Aaron and was having his tummy rubbed when Stevie looked up from his blocks. Aaron noticed the child's stare and smiled.

"Hey there, little man, what's up?" he asked the autistic child.

The child's change of expression could be described like the sun burning through a thick haze of storm clouds. His usually blank face became animated as his eyes twinkled with the light of awareness. A smile so bright and wide spread across Stevie's face that Aaron was genuinely warmed by its intensity.

"Bootiful," Stevie said, holding out his hand.

"Stevie?" Lori questioned, her paperback falling to the floor. "Tommy, look at Stevie."

But the sound of his son's voice had already pulled Tom away from the movie. They both slid from their seats to the floor and watched as their child gently touched Aaron's cheek with a tiny hand, a smile still radiating from his usually expressionless face.

"Bootiful," the child repeated. "Bootiful."

Then, as quickly as awareness had appeared, it was gone, the clouds again covering up the sun.

Stevie showed no sign that he even remembered what he had just done. He simply returned his attention to his blocks.

"He spoke to you," his mother said, grabbing Aaron by the shoulders and squeezing excitedly. "He actually spoke to you."

Tommy kneeled by his son, grinning from ear to ear. "What do you think it means?" the big man asked, his voice filled with emotion. "He hasn't said a word in two years." He touched the boy's head lovingly. "That would be something, wouldn't it?" he wondered aloud, his eyes never leaving Stevie. "If he started to talk again."

Both parents began to play with the child and his blocks, hoping to elicit another verbal response. Something, anything to prove that the boy's sudden reaction wasn't just a fluke.

Stevie remained in his world of silence.

Aaron got up. "Do you want an apple?" he asked Gabriel.

The dog sprang to his feet and wagged his tail. *"Apple, oh yes,"* he said. *"Hungry, yes. Apple."*

As they left the room Aaron couldn't shake the uncomfortable feeling that Stevie's behavior was somehow connected to the bizarreness that had been affecting his life since his birthday. *So much for distraction,* he thought as he took an apple from the small wicker basket atop the microwave and brought it to the cutting board on the counter.

"Did you see the way he looked at me?" Aaron asked the dog as he took a knife from the dish strainer by the sink and split the fruit in half. "It was like he was seeing something—something other than me."

"Bootiful," Gabriel responded, gazing up by his side. *"He said bootiful."*

Aaron cut the core out, then cut half of the apple into strips.

"The way he looked at me, it was like the old man at the common."

He fed the dog a slice of apple, which Gabriel eagerly devoured.

Aaron saw the old man in his mind pointing at him. *"You are Nephilim,"* he had said.

"First I'm Nephilim and now I'm bootiful," he said to himself as he leaned against the counter.

"More apple?" Gabriel asked, a tendril of thick drool streaming from his jowls to the floor.

Aaron gave him a slice and took one for himself. Something weird was happening to him. And he realized that he had no other choice than to find out exactly what that was.

He took another bite of the apple, then gave the rest to Gabriel.

It was a crazy idea, but he was desperate to know what was happening to him. He would have to take a chance. Before his appointment with Dr. Jonas the next day, he would try to find the old man from the common.

"Hey, Gabriel," he asked the dog, who was still chewing, "do you want to go to the common with me tomorrow?"

The dog swallowed and gazed up at him. *"More apple?"* he asked.

Aaron shook his head. "No. Apple's gone."

The dog seemed to think for a moment and then gave his answer.

"No apple. Then go to common."

What was I thinking? Aaron scowled to himself. He pulled back and let the tennis ball fly.

Gabriel bounded across the common in hot pursuit of the bouncing ball. *"Get ball,"* he heard the dog say in an excited, breathless voice as he grew closer to capturing the fluorescent yellow prize.

It was a beautiful spring morning, with just the hint of winter's cold that had only begrudgingly begun to recede a few short weeks ago.

The wind still had a sharpness to it and he zipped his brown leather jacket a little higher.

Gabriel cavorted with the ball clenched tightly in his mouth.

Since his strange ability to communicate with the dog manifested, Aaron was amazed at how little it took to make Gabriel truly happy: a scratch above his tail, a piece of cheese, calling him a good boy. Simplicity. *It must be pretty awesome to get so much from so little,* he mused as he watched the dog gallop toward him.

"Give me that ball," Aaron demanded, playfully lowering himself into a menacing crouch.

Gabriel growled; the muscles in his back legs twitched with anticipation.

Aaron lunged and the dog bolted to avoid capture.

"C'mere, you crazy dog," he said with a laugh, and began to chase the animal.

There was a part of him that really wasn't too disappointed they hadn't seen the old-timer. It meant a reprieve from serious thoughts of recent events, the weird questions with probably equally weird answers that he wasn't quite sure he was ready to hear.

He snagged Gabriel by the choke chain around his neck and pulled the growling beast toward him. "Gotcha," he said as he leaned close to the dog's face. "Now I'm gonna take that ball!"

Gabriel's growl grew louder, higher, more excited as he struggled to free himself. Aaron grabbed the spit-covered ball and pried it free from the dog's mouth.

"The prize is mine!" Aaron proclaimed as he held the dripping ball aloft.

"Not prize," Gabriel said, able to talk again now that the ball had been removed. *"Just ball."*

Aaron wrinkled his nose in revulsion as he studied the slime-covered ball in his hand. "And what a ball it is," he said.

He watched the dog's head move from side to side as he tossed the tennis ball from one hand to the other. "Bet you want this bad," he teased.

"Want ball bad," Gabriel responded, mesmerized by its movement.

Aaron made a move to throw it, hiding the ball beneath his arm, and the dog shot off in hot pursuit of nothing.

He laughed as he watched Gabriel searching the ground, even looking up into the air just in case it hadn't fallen to earth yet.

"Yoohoo!" he called to the dog. And as Gabriel looked in his direction, he held the ball up. "Looking for this?"

Surprised, the dog charged back toward him. *"How you get ball back?"* he asked with amazement.

Aaron smiled. "Magic," he said and chuckled.

"Magic," Gabriel repeated in a soft, canine whisper of wonderment, his eyes still stuck to the ball.

The dog suddenly became distracted by

something beyond Aaron. *"Who that?"* he asked.

"Who's who?" Aaron turned around.

At first he didn't recognize the man sitting on the bench across the common, soaking up the sunshine. But then the man waved, and he suddenly knew. Aaron felt his heart beat faster, questions turning through his mind, questions he wasn't entirely certain he wanted answered.

"What wrong?" Gabriel asked, concern in his voice.

"Nothing," Aaron said, not taking his eyes from the man on the bench.

"Then why afraid?"

Aaron looked down at the dog, startled by the question. "I'm not afraid," he said, insulted by the dog's insinuation.

The dog looked at him and then across the common. *"Afraid of stranger?"*

"I told you I am not afraid," Aaron said anxiously, and began to head toward the man.

"Smell afraid," the dog stressed as he followed by his side.

They were about six feet away when Gabriel moved ahead of him, his head tilted back as he sniffed the air. *"Man smell old,"* he said. *"Old and different,"* he added between drafts of air.

Aaron could see that the man was smiling, his long wispy, white hair moving around his head in the cool, spring breeze.

"Beautiful day," the old man said in English, rather than the ancient language he'd been speaking when they first met.

Gabriel ran at the man, tail wagging.

"Gabriel, no!" Aaron ordered, speeding up to catch the dog. "Get over here."

The dog leaped up, putting his two front paws on the bench, and began to lick the stranger's face as if they were old friends.

"Hello, I Gabriel," he said as he licked and sniffed at the man's face, neck, and ears. *"Who you?"*

"My name is Ezekiel, but you can call me Zeke," the man answered as he patted the dog's soft yellow head.

"Are you telling me or the dog?" Aaron asked as he took Gabriel by the collar and gently pulled him away. "Get down, Gabriel," he said sharply. "Behave."

The dog went silent, bowing his head, embarrassed that he had been scolded.

"He asked me what my name was and I told him," Zeke said as he sat back on the bench and smiled at the dog. "He's a beautiful animal. You're very lucky to have him."

Aaron stroked Gabriel's head in an attempt to keep the excitable animal calm. He laughed at the old man and smiled slyly. "So the dog spoke to you?"

Zeke smiled back. "You spoke the language of the messenger to me yesterday," he said, folding his arms across his chest. "Don't tell me you can't understand the dog."

Aaron felt as if he had been slapped; a hot, tingling sweat erupted at the base of his neck and shoulder blades. "Who . . . who are you?" he asked—not the best of questions, but the only one he could dredge up at the moment.

"Zeke," Gabriel answered helpfully, pulling away from Aaron to lick at the man's hands. *"Zeke, Aaron. He Zeke."*

Zeke smiled and reached out to rub beneath the dog's chin. "He's right, aren't you?" he asked the panting animal. "I'm Zeke and you are—what did he call you? Aaron?"

The old man wiped the dog's slobber on his pant leg and extended his hand toward Aaron. He hesitated at first, but then took Zeke's hand in his and they shook.

"I'm very pleased to meet you, Aaron. Sorry about yesterday. Did I scare you?"

Their hands came apart and Aaron shrugged. "Wasn't so much scaring as confusing the hell out of me."

Zeke nodded in understanding and continued to pet Gabriel. "I bet it's been pretty strange for you the last couple a' days."

Questions screamed to be asked, but Aaron kept them at bay, choosing to let the old man reveal what he knew at a natural pace. He didn't want to appear too eager.

"And how do you know that?"

The old man tilted his head back, closed his eyes, and sniffed the air.

"How do I know that summer's right around the corner?" he asked, letting the morning sunshine bathe his grizzled, unshaven features.

The man didn't appear as old as Aaron originally had thought, probably in his early sixties, but there was something about him—in his eyes, in the way he carried himself—that made Aaron think he was much older.

"It's in the air, boy," Zeke said. "I can smell it."

"Okay," Aaron said. "You could smell that I was having a bad time. That makes sense."

Zeke nodded. "Kinda, sorta. I could smell that you were changing, and just assumed that you were probably having some problems with it."

Aaron had put the tennis ball inside his jacket pocket and now slowly removed it. Gabriel's eyes bugged like something out of a Warner Brothers cartoon. "I can't believe I'm having this conversation," he said as he showed the ball to Gabriel and threw it across the common. "Go play."

Gabriel ran off in pursuit. They watched the dog in silence. Aaron wanted to leave—but something kept him there. Perhaps it was the chance of an explanation.

"What happened first?" Zeke asked, breaking the silence. "Was it the language thing? Did the dog start talking and you thought you'd lost all your marbles?"

Aaron didn't want to answer but found it

was impossible to hold back. "Kids at school were speaking Portuguese. I don't know how to speak Portuguese, but suddenly I could understand them perfectly fine, like they were speaking English."

Zeke nodded with understanding. "Doesn't matter anymore what language somebody is talking," he said. "You'll be able to understand and speak it as if it were your native tongue. It's one of the perks."

Gabriel was running in a circle. *"I got the ball!"* he yelled, diving at the tennis ball lying in the grass and sending it rolling. He pounced on it with tireless vigor.

"The language doesn't even have to be human, as you've probably guessed by now." The old man looked at him. "Wait until you hear what a tree sloth has to say."

"It's insane," Aaron muttered.

"Not really," Zeke responded. "They just have a unique way of looking at things."

Aaron was confused. "What? Who has a unique way of looking at things?" he asked.

"Tree sloths," Zeke answered.

"I wasn't talking about sloths," Aaron said, growing agitated.

"Oh, you were talking about all this with the languages and stuff?" Zeke asked. "Well, you'd better get used to it 'cause it's what you are," the old man said matter of factly.

Aaron turned from watching his dog play

and faced the man. "Get used to being insane? I don't think—"

Zeke shook his head and held up his hands. "Not insane," he said. "Nephilim. It's what you are; you don't have a choice."

There was that word again. The word that had disobediently bounced around inside Aaron's skull since he first heard it, impossible to forget—like it didn't want to be lost.

"Why do you keep calling me that?" he asked, tension coiling in his voice as he readied himself for the answer.

The old man ran both hands through his wild, white hair. Then he leaned forward and rested his elbows on his knees. "The Nephilim are the children of angels and—"

"Angels and human women," Aaron interrupted. He didn't want to waste any time hearing things he already knew. "I know that; I looked it up in the library. Now tell me what the hell it has to do with *me.*"

"It's kind of complicated," Zeke said. "If you give me half a second and let me speak, I might be able to clear some things up."

He stared at Aaron, a stare both intense and calming, a stare that suggested this was not a typical, crazy old man, but someone who was once a figure of authority.

Gabriel had wandered over to a newly planted tree and was sniffing the spring mulch spread at its base.

"I'm sorry," Aaron said. "Go on."

Zeke stroked his unshaven chin, mentally found his place, and began again. "Okay, the Nephilim are the children of angels and mortal women. Not too common really, the mothers have a real difficult time bringing the babies to term—never mind surviving the delivery. But every once in a while, a Nephilim child survives."

Gabriel had returned and dropped the ball, now covered in the fragrant mulch, at Zeke's feet. *"Look, Zeke, ball."*

Zeke reached down and picked it up, turning it over in his hands as Gabriel stared attentively.

"They're something all right, part heavenly host, part human, a blending of the Almighty's most impressive creations."

The old man bounced the ball once, and then again. The dog's head bobbed up and down as he watched it.

"Nephilim usually have a normal childhood, but once they reach a certain level of maturity, the angelic nature starts to assert itself. That's when the problems begin, almost as if the two halves no longer get along." Zeke threw the ball and Gabriel was off. "Seems to happen around eighteen or nineteen."

Aaron felt the color drain from his face, and he turned to the old man on the bench. "You're trying to tell me that . . . that my mother . . . my mother slept with an angel? For Christ's sake!"

Gabriel returned with the ball and stopped at Aaron, sensing his master's growing unease. The dog sniffed at his leg, determined that things were fine and went to Zeke.

"Did you know your father?" Zeke asked, idly picking up the ball.

"It doesn't matter," Aaron barked, and turned his back on the old man and his dog.

He could see his car parked across the street and wanted to run for it. He could feel himself begin to slip—teetering on the brink of an emotional roller coaster. Zeke's question had hit him with the force of a sledgehammer. His mother had died giving birth to him, and the identity of his father went with her.

"That's where you're wrong, Aaron," Zeke said from behind him. "It does matter."

Aaron faced him. He suddenly felt weak, drained of energy.

"There is a choir of angels called the Powers. They are the oldest of the angels, the first created by God."

Gabriel had caught sight of some seagulls. *"Big birds,"* he grumbled, and began to creep stealthily toward them like some fearsome predator.

Zeke stood up and moved toward Aaron. "I want you to listen to me very carefully," he said, holding him in that powerful stare. "The Powers are kinda like—" He stopped to think a moment. "The Powers are like secret police, like God's storm troopers. It's their job to destroy what they believe is offensive to the Creator."

Aaron was confused. "I don't understand," he said, shaking his head.

"The Powers decided long ago that Nephilim are offensive. A blight before the eyes of God."

"The Powers kill them?" Aaron asked, already knowing the answer.

Zeke nodded slowly, his expression dire. "In the beginning it was a slaughter; most of the ones killed were still just children. They didn't even know why they had to die." The old man reached out and grabbed Aaron's arm in a powerful grip. "I want you to listen very carefully because your life might depend on it."

Zeke's grip was firm and it had begun to hurt. Aaron tried to pull away, but the man's strength held him tight.

"It's still going on today, Aaron. Do you understand what I'm saying to you? Nephilim are still being born, and when they begin to show signs of their true nature, the Powers find them."

Aaron finally yanked his arm free. "Let go of me," he snarled.

"The Powers find them and *kill* them. They have no mercy. In their eyes, you're a freak of nature, something that should never have been allowed to happen."

Aaron was suddenly very afraid. "I have to go," he told the man, scanning the common for his dog. He whistled and saw Gabriel in the distance lifting his leg against a trash barrel. The dog began to trot in their direction.

"You have to listen to me, Aaron," Zeke warned. "Your abilities are blossoming. If you're not careful—"

Aaron whirled and stepped toward the old man, fists clenched in suppressed fury. He couldn't hold it back anymore. He was scared—scared and very angry for he was starting to believe Zeke's wild story. He wanted answers, but not these—these were a ticket to a locked ward.

"What?" he screamed. "If I'm not careful these storm trooper angels are going to fly down out of the sky and kill me?" Aaron suddenly thought of his dream, the recurring nightmare, and wanted to vomit. It made him all the angrier.

"I know it sounds insane," Zeke said, "but you've got to understand. This has been going on for thousands of years and—"

"Shut up!" Aaron exploded in the old man's face. "Just shut your stupid mouth!" He began to walk away, then stopped and turned back. "And how do you know all this, Zeke?" he asked, sticking his finger in the man's face. "How do you know about Nephilim and Powers and the killing?"

The old man looked perfectly calm as he spoke. "I think you already know the answer to that, and if you don't—think a bit harder."

Aaron laughed out loud, a cruel sound and it surprised him. "Let me guess. You're a Nephilim too?"

Zeke smiled sadly and shook his head. "Not a Nephilim," he said, and began to unbutton his threadbare raincoat. He was wearing a loose-fitting green sweater beneath and some faded jeans. "I'm a fallen angel, a Grigori, if you want to be specific," he said as he moved closer.

He yanked on the collar of his sweater, pulling it down over his right shoulder to expose unusually pale flesh—and something more. A strange, fleshy protrusion, about six inches long, jutted from the old man's shoulder blade. It was covered in what appeared to be a fine coat of white hairs—no, on closer examination it wasn't hair at all—it was covered in downy, white feathers. Aaron jumped back as the protrusion began to move up and down in a flapping motion. Something similar on the other shoulder moved in unison beneath the sweater.

"What the hell is it?" Aaron asked, both fascinated and disgusted by the wagging, vestigial appendage.

"It's all I've got left of them," Zeke said softly, an almost palpable sadness emanating from him in waves. "It's all that's left of my wings."

chapter five

"Y'know what, I've had enough," Aaron said as he threw up his hands and backed away from Zeke. "I'm done."

He felt as though he were falling farther and farther into the depths of insanity, only with Zeke's addition, he had a buddy for the trip. Even the voice of reason inside his head was beginning to come undone. *Maybe it is all true,* he thought. *What else could those things be on his back but the stumps of wings . . .* He wanted to slap himself for thinking it. *No way. It would be better if it were a brain tumor making me understand these languages—making me think that my dog is talking to me. That would make it easier,* he reasoned. Then he could brush off the old man as just another lunatic.

Aaron called again for his dog. "C'mon, Gabriel," he said, clapping his hands together. "Let's go for a ride."

He continued to walk away from the crazy old man, and his equally crazy delusions.

"Aaron, please," Zeke pleaded. "I have more to tell you—to show you. Aaron?"

He didn't turn around. He couldn't allow himself to be ensnared in this madness. Yes, Zeke was pretty convincing and knew all the right buttons to push, but angels? It was just too much for Aaron to swallow. Space aliens, maybe—angels, not a chance. He would see Dr. Jonas later today and then set up an appointment with the doctor's friend at Mass General. Between the two of them, a rational explanation for his condition—*could it actually be called a condition?* he wondered—a rational explanation for his current situation would be found. At this stage of the game a tumor might not even be so bad. At least it was some kind of concrete explanation that he could accept, understand, and deal with.

Angels. Absolutely friggin' ridiculous.

Aaron looked down to see if Gabriel still had his ball. It was the Lab's favorite toy, and Aaron could see himself here at ten o'clock tonight with a flashlight searching for it.

The dog wasn't with him.

He looked around the common. Had the dog become distracted, as he so often did, by a squirrel or a bird or an interesting smell in the grass?

Aaron caught sight of him on the other side of the common where a section of the pipe fence was missing. The dog was standing with Zeke. He took a few steps toward them and wondered how they could have gotten way over there so fast.

"Hey, Gabriel," he called, cupping his hands around his mouth to amplify his voice. "C'mon, pup, let's go for a ride."

The dog didn't pay him the least bit of attention. He was standing attentively alongside Zeke, staring up at the man with his tail wagging. An uncomfortable feeling began somewhere in the pit of Aaron's stomach. He'd felt like this in the past, usually right before something bad happened. He remembered a time not too long ago when he had experienced a similar feeling and discovered that Stevie had turned on the hot water in the bathtub when nobody was looking. If he hadn't searched out the source of his uneasiness, the child would surely have scalded himself badly. Aaron felt kind of like he did then—only worse.

Aaron began walking toward them. "Gabriel, come here," he said in his sternest voice. "Come."

The dog glanced his way briefly but was distracted as the old man held up the ball for Gabriel to see. Zeke looked in Aaron's direction, ball held aloft.

The awful feeling squirming in his gut got worse and Aaron began to jog toward them—and then to run.

Zeke looked toward the street outside the common, checking it out as if getting ready to cross. It was getting later in the morning and the traffic had begun to pick up. Zeke again showed the ball to Gabriel and Aaron could see the dog's posture tense in anticipation.

"Hey!" Aaron yelled, his voice cracking. He was almost there, no farther than twenty feet away.

The old man looked into the traffic and then to Aaron. "I'm sorry," Zeke said, raising his voice.

Panic gripped him and Aaron began to run faster. "Gabriel!" he yelled at the top of his lungs. "Gabriel, look at me!"

The dog paid him no mind, his dark eyes mesmerized by the power of the ball. Aaron was almost there.

"There's no other way," he heard the old man say as he again studied the flow of oncoming traffic—and threw the ball into the street.

Aaron saw it as though watching a slow-motion scene in a movie. The tennis ball left the old man's hand and sailed through the air. He heard a voice that must have been his screaming "Gabriel, *no*!" as the dog followed the arc of the ball and jumped. The ball bounced once and Gabriel was there, ready to snatch it up in his mouth, when the white Ford Escort struck him broadside and sent him sailing through the air as though weightless.

They were the most sickening sounds Aaron had ever heard, brakes screeching as tires fought for purchase on Tarmac, followed by the dull thud of a thick rubber bumper connecting with fur, flesh, and bone. His slow-motion perception abruptly ended as Gabriel's limp body hit the street in a twisted heap.

"Oh my God—no!" Aaron screamed as he ran to his pet.

He fell to his knees beside the animal. *There's so much blood,* he thought. It stained the Lab's beautiful yellow coat and oozed from the corners of his mouth. It had even begun to seep out along the ground from somewhere beneath his body.

Aaron carefully wrapped his arms around his best friend. "Oh God, oh God, oh God, oh God," he cried as he pressed his face to the dog's side.

He placed an ear against the still-warm fur and listened for a heartbeat. But the sounds of horns from backed-up traffic and the murmur from curious bystanders was all he could discern.

"Will you shut up!" he screamed at the top of his lungs, lifting his head from the dog's side.

Gabriel shuddered violently. *He's still alive.* Tears of joy streamed from Aaron's eyes as he bent down to whisper in his friend's ear. "Don't you worry, boy, I'm here. Everything is going to be fine."

"Aaron?" Gabriel asked, his voice a weak whimper.

"Shhhhh, you be quiet now," he told the dog in a calming tone. "I've got you. You're going to be all right."

He stroked the dog's blood-stained fur, not sure if he believed what he was saying. He wanted to fall apart, to scream, rant, and rave, but knew that he had to keep control. He had to save Gabriel.

"Aaron . . . Aaron, hurt bad," Gabriel croaked, and began to spasm as frothy pink blood bubbled from his mouth.

"Hang on, pal, hang on, boy. I'm going to help you."

Aaron tried to pick him up, and Gabriel let out a heartrending shriek so filled with pain that it affected him like a physical blow.

"What do I do?" he asked aloud, panic beginning to override a cool head. "He's dying. What do I do?"

The thought of praying strayed into his head, and he was considering doing just that when he realized that he wasn't even sure how.

"If you want Gabriel to live, you must listen to me," said a voice from behind.

Aaron turned to see Zeke standing over him.

"Get away from me, you son of a bitch!" he spat. "You *did* this! You did this to him!"

"Listen to me," Zeke hissed close to his ear. "If you don't want him to die, you'll do as I say."

For the first time Aaron felt as if he couldn't

go on. Even after all he had been through, caught up in the merciless current of the foster care system, he never gave up hope that eventually it would turn out for the best. But now, as he gazed at his best friend dying in the street, he wasn't sure.

"Aaron," Zeke shouted for his attention. "Do you want him to bleed to death on this dirty street? Do you?"

He turned to look at the man, tears running down his face. "No," he managed. "I want him to live. Please . . . please, help him. . . ."

"Not me," Zeke said with a shake of his head. "You. You're going to help Gabriel."

The old man knelt beside him. "We don't have a moment to spare," he said, looking upon the dying animal. "Lay your hands on him—quickly now."

Aaron did as he was told, and placed the palms of both hands on the dog's side.

"Now close your eyes," the old man instructed.

"But we can't—" Aaron started to protest.

"Close your eyes, damn it!" Zeke commanded him.

Aaron did as he was told, his hands still upon Gabriel's body. The dog's flesh seemed to have grown colder, and he grew desperate. The noise around them receded.

"Please, Zeke," he begged as Gabriel's life slipped agonizingly away.

"It's not up to me now," the old man said. "It's up to you."

"I don't understand. If we can get him to a vet maybe . . ."

"A vet can't help him. He'll be dead in a couple a' minutes if you don't do something," Zeke said. "You gotta let it out, Aaron."

"Let what out? . . . I don't understand."

"What's to understand? It's there, inside you, waiting. It's been there since you were born—just waiting for its time."

Aaron sobbed, letting his chin drop to his chest. "I . . . I don't know what you're saying."

"No time for crying, boy. Look for it in the darkness. It's there, I can smell it on you. Look closely. Can you see it?"

Gabriel is going to die, Aaron realized as he knelt by the animal, hands laid upon him, feeling him slip away. There was no way around it. The old man was delusional and dangerous. He debated whether he should hold the man for the police—imagine if Gabriel had been a child. It might be best for the old man to be behind bars or at least in a hospital where he could receive the proper care.

Aaron was about to open his eyes when he felt it stir inside his mind, and he saw something. In the darkness it was there, something he'd never seen before.

And it was moving toward him. *Is this what the old man is talking about?* he asked himself near panic. How did he know it would be there? What was it? What was coming at him through the blackness behind his eyes?

"I . . . I see something," he said with disbelief. "What should I do?"

"Call to it, Aaron," Zeke cautioned, "not with your voice, but with your mind. Welcome it, let it know that it's needed."

Aaron did as he was told, and reached out with his mind. He couldn't make out exactly what it was, its shape kept changing—but it seemed to be some kind of animal—and it was moving inexorably closer.

"Hello?" he thought, feeling foolish, yet desperate to try anything. *"Can . . . can you hear me?"* Was it all some bizarre figment of his imagination brought on by the stress of the situation? he wondered.

It was a mouse scrambling through the darkness toward him, a mouse with fur so white that it seemed to glow.

"I have no idea what I'm supposed to do—or what you are—but I'm willing to try anything to help my friend."

The mouse stopped, its beady black eyes seeming to touch him. It reared back on its haunches, as if considering his words, and then began to groom itself.

"Do . . . do you understand me?" he asked the tiny creature with the power of his thoughts.

It was no longer a mouse, and Aaron gasped.

The mouse had become an owl, its feathers the color of snow, and before he could wrap his brain around what had just happened, it changed again. From an owl it turned into an albino toad—and from the toad, a white rabbit. The thing inside his head was now morphing its shape at a blinding rate; from mammal to insect, from bird to fish. But though its form continued to alter, its eyes remained the same. There was an awesome intelligence in those deep, black eyes, and something more—recognition. It knew him, and somehow, he knew it.

It had become a snake—a cobra—and it reared back on its bone-colored muscular shaft of a body, swaying from side to side, its mouth open in a fearsome hiss as it readied to strike.

"I don't like this, Zeke," Aaron said aloud, eyes still tightly closed. "You have to tell me what to do."

"Don't be afraid, Aaron. It's a part of you. It's been a part of you since you were conceived," Zeke counseled. "But you have to hurry. Gabriel doesn't have much time left."

"I don't know what to do!" he cried as a humming-bird fluttered before him.

"Talk to it," Zeke barked. "And do as you're told."

"My dog is dying." Aaron directed his thoughts toward the shape-changing creature floating before him in a sea of pitch. *"In fact he might already be dead, but I can't give up. Please, can you help me?*

Is there anything you can do to help me save him?"

It had become a fetus that looked vaguely human. It simply hovered there in its membranous sack, unresponsive, its dark eyes fixed upon him.

Aaron was angry. Time was running out, and here he was talking to some fetal figment of his troubled state of mind.

"I've had enough," his thoughts screamed. *"If you're going to help me, do it. If not, get the hell out of my mind and let me get him to a vet."*

Like a ship changing course, the child-thing slowly turned, shifted its shape to some kind of fish, and began to swim away.

"It's . . . it's leaving, Zeke."

Aaron felt the man's hand roughly upon his shoulder. "You can't allow it to go. Talk to it, Aaron. Beg it to come back. Whether you're ready or not, it's the only way that Gabriel will survive."

"Please," Aaron projected into the sea of black. *"Please don't let him die, I . . . I don't know what I'd do without him."*

The fish, now an iguana, continued on its way. A luminous bat, and then a centipede, the force within his mind receded, growing smaller with distance. Aaron wasn't sure why he did what he did next.

In the ancient language first spoken to him by Zeke, what the old man had called the language of messengers, he called out once more to the thing in his mind.

"Please, help me," he thought in that arcane tongue. *"If it is in your power, please don't let my friend die."*

At first he didn't think his pleas had any effect—but then he saw that a chimpanzee had turned and was slowly returning with a comical gait.

"It's coming back," Aaron said to Zeke, not in English, but in the old tongue.

"Open yourself to it," he responded in kind. *"Take it into yourself. Accept it as part of you."*

Aaron shook his head violently, eyes still clamped shut. *"What does that mean?"* he asked.

The old man dug his nails painfully into his shoulders. *"Accept it, or you both die."*

A jungle cat was almost upon him, and Aaron gazed into the fearsome beast's eyes.

"I accept you," he thought in the ancient speak, unsure of what he should be saying, and the panther lifted its head to become a serpent, but this was unlike any snake he had ever seen before. It had tufts of silky fine hair flowing from parts of its tubular body, and small muscular limbs that clawed at the air as if in anticipation. And the strangest and most disturbing thing of all, it had a face—something not usually associated with the look of a reptile. This serpent wore an expression on its unusual facial features, one of contentment, and spread its malformed arms, beckoning in a gesture that suggested Aaron, too, had been accepted.

The ophidian beast began to glow eerily, and Aaron could discern a fine webwork of veins and capillaries running throughout the creature's body. The light of the snake became blinding and the solid black behind his eyes was burned away like night with the approach of dawn.

A painful surge of energy that felt like thousands of volts of electricity suddenly coursed through Aaron's body. He opened his eyes and looked down on his dog. He knew that Gabriel's life was almost at an end.

"It's time, Aaron," he heard Zeke say.

Aaron looked at him. For some reason the old man was crying. Aaron's hands tingled painfully and he gazed down at them. A white crackling energy, like eruptions of arc lightning, danced from one fingertip to the next.

"What's happening to me?" he asked breathlessly.

"You're whole now, Aaron. You're complete."

Instinctively Aaron knew what had to be done. Gazing at his hands, he turned them palms down and again placed them upon Gabriel. He felt the energy leave his body, leaping from his fingers to the dog, burrowing beneath fur and flesh. And the air around them was filled with the charged scent of ozone.

Gabriel's body twitched and thrashed, but Aaron did not take his hands away. The blood that spattered the dog's fur started to dry, to smolder, evaporating into oily wisps that snaked into the air.

"I think you've done all you can," Zeke said quietly nearby.

Aaron pulled his hands away from the animal. For a brief moment his handprints glowed white upon the dog's fur—and then were gone. The powerful sensation throughout his body was fading, but he still felt different, both mentally and physically.

"What did I do?" he asked, looking from Zeke to the dog.

Gabriel was breathing slow regular breaths, as if he were merely taking a little snooze.

"What needed to be done if Gabriel—and you—are to survive," Zeke answered ominously.

Aaron reached out and touched the dog's head. "Gabriel?" he said softly, not sure if he believed what he was seeing.

Gabriel languidly lifted his head from the street, yawned, and fixed Aaron in his gaze. *"Hello, Aaron,"* he said as he rolled onto his belly.

Aaron could feel his eyes well up with emotion. He leaned forward and hugged the dog. "Are you all right?" he asked, squeezing the animal's neck and planting a kiss on the side of his muzzle.

"I'm fine, Aaron," Gabriel answered. The dog seemed distracted, pulling away from his embrace.

"What's the matter?" Aaron asked the dog as he looked around.

"Have you seen my ball?" Gabriel asked in a voice filled with surprising intelligence.

And Aaron came to the frightening realization that he may not have been the only one to change.

Too late, the angel Camael thought, perched like a gargoyle at the edge of the building. He sadly gazed down at a restaurant consumed in flames. *Too late to save another.*

Thick gray smoke billowed from the broken front windows of Eddy's Breakfast and Lunch; tongues of orange flame, like things alive, reached out from the heart of the conflagration, hoping to ensnare something, anything to fuel its ravenous hunger.

From his roost across the street, Camael watched as firefighters aimed their hoses and tried to suffocate the inferno with water before it had a chance to spread to neighboring structures. They would need to be persistent, the angel thought, for it was a most unnatural fire they battled this morn.

He had planned to make contact with the girl this very morning, to guide her through the change her body was undergoing, and warn her of the dangers it presented—dangers that came far sooner than even he had imagined.

Camael had been watching the girl—*What was her name? Susan.*

He had been observing Susan since he first caught scent of her imminent transformation. It was so much harder to track them these days; the world was a much larger and more complex place than it had been in the beginning. The enemy used trackers, human hounds, but he could not bear to use the oft-pathetic creatures in that way. Camael found it far too cruel.

Susan was a loner, as was often the nature of the breed, living alone without close friends or family. But she did have a job as a waitress, a job that seemed to be the center of her reality. That was where she came alive: surrounded by the chattering masses of the popular eating establishment. She would serve them, converse with them, and send them on their way back into the world with a kind word and a wave. At Eddy's she was accepted, loved even; but outside its doors was a cold, harsh, unfriendly place.

Camael had watched and waited for the signs of change in her. He had even started to frequent the restaurant just so that he might observe her more closely. He didn't have long to wait. Her appearance became disheveled, dark circles forming beneath her eyes, an obvious sign that she was not sleeping. The dreams were usually first, the collective memories of an entire race from thousands of years attempting to assert themselves. That alone was enough to drive some of them mad, never mind the changes that were still to come.

The firefighters below seemed to have the blaze under control and were entering the building, most likely to retrieve the bodies of those who had been trapped within.

Camael sighed heavily. At this early hour Eddy's would have been crowded with customers—those coming off the late shift and those just beginning their workday. *Verchiel certainly outdid himself this time,* the angel thought as the first of the victims was carried from the smoldering building.

The girl must have been much further along than Camael had realized if they were able to find her with such ease. If only he had acted earlier this might have been avoided. He might have been able to convince the young woman to run before the Powers had a chance to lock on to her scent.

He would need to move faster with the next.

The firefighters were laying the smoking bodies down behind a hastily constructed screen on the sidewalk in front of the burnt-out shell that had once been Eddy's. Camael counted sixteen so far. The girl's had yet to be recovered.

There was a ferocity to the Powers' latest attacks, a complete lack of concern for innocent lives, a certain desperation to their actions. He thought of Samchia's murder in Hong Kong. There had always been killing, it was what the

Powers did—it was their reason for existence. But of late . . . Why this sudden escalation of violence? It disturbed him. What had stirred the hornet's nest, so to speak?

A frightening thought invaded his consciousness. What if she had been the One? What if Susan was the One foretold of in a prophecy thousands of years old?

Camael recalled the moment that had altered his chosen path as if it had happened only moments before. They had descended from the heavens on the ancient city of Urkish, the overpowering desire to eradicate evil spurring them on. It was rumored that the city was a haven for the unclean, a place where those who offended God could thrive in secret. The Powers were on a holy mission, and all who stood against them fell before their righteousness.

In a hovel made of mud and straw they found him, an old man, a seer, one of his eyes covered by a milky caul. He was surrounded by clay tablets upon which something had been written—a prophecy. It was Camael's former captain, Verchiel, who first read the seer's scrawl. His words foretold of the melding of human and angel, and how that joining would sire an offspring—an offspring more than human, more than angel, who would be the key to reuniting those who had fallen from Heaven with their most holy Father.

"Blasphemy!" the captain of the Powers had

screamed as he shattered the tablets beneath his heel.

And on that day, all trace of the city of Urkish was wiped from the planet and from history.

But not the words—try as he might, Camael could not forget the seer's words. They spoke of a promise, of a more peaceful time when his existence would not be one filled with the passing of judgment and the meting out of death. The words were what made him abandon his brethren and their holy mission so very long ago. Words that still haunted him today.

But what if Susan had been the One? It was a question he struggled with every time he was too late to save one of them. What if she had been the key to reuniting the fallen with Heaven? What if Verchiel had taken it all away in a self-righteous burst of purifying fire?

Camael finally saw Susan's body among the last to be carried from the fire-ravaged building. Her blackened limbs reached up to the heavens, as if pleading to be saved.

It pained him that he had not been there for her.

What if she . . . a tiny voice in the back of his mind began to ask and he promptly silenced it. He couldn't think that way. He had to keep going or all his past sacrifices would be for naught.

Camael turned from the carnage and strode

across the rooftop. The angel tipped his head back to the early morning sun and sniffed the air.

There were others, others who needed him.

With the Powers' attacks on the rise, he would need to move quickly if any were to be saved.

Zeke motioned for Aaron to sit. There was one chair in the tiny room, a black leather office chair that had probably been rescued from the garbage. A large swath of gray electrical tape ran down the middle of the seat and Aaron touched it to see if it was sticky before he sat.

After the business at the common, the three had quickly left the scene to avoid unwanted questions. The driver of the white Escort seemed genuinely pleased that she hadn't killed Gabriel, and had even petted the dog before driving off. As the crowd rapidly dispersed Zeke suggested they head for his place.

It was a fifteen-minute walk to the Osmond Hotel, a boardinghouse on Washington Street, not too far from downtown Lynn. Because Gabriel was with them, and pets were not allowed in the Osmond, they went around back and entered through the emergency exit held open with a cinder block for cross ventilation.

Zeke lived on the fourth floor, room 416, of the dilapidated building. It wasn't the kind of place where one would expect to find an angel.

"A fallen angel," Zeke corrected as he sat

down on the single-size bed covered by a green, moth-eaten army blanket. "There's a big difference."

Aaron had bought sodas and a bottle of water for Gabriel in a bodega they had passed on the way to the rooming house. "Do you have something I can put this in?" he asked as he cracked the seal on the water.

Zeke got up and started rummaging through plastic trash bags that littered the floor. "Sorry, I don't," he said. "Can't cook in the room so there's no reason for me to have any dishes."

Aaron poured some water into his cupped hand and offered it to the dog. "It's okay. We'll manage."

"Thank you," Gabriel said in a well-mannered voice. He dropped his ball between his paws and began to lap the liquid from his master's hand.

Zeke lay back on the bed and popped the top on his soda can. "You all right?" he asked Aaron as he fished for something in the pockets of his tattered trench coat.

Gabriel finished his water. *"Thank you again, Aaron,"* he said, and licked his chops. *"I was very thirsty."*

Aaron wiped the slobber on his pant leg. "Yeah, I'm fine," he said to Zeke, popping the top on his own drink. His eyes never left the dog. "Does he seem—I don't know—smarter to you?"

Zeke produced a nip of Seagram's from his

pocket and poured the contents into his can of soda. "Not supposed to have booze in here either," he said with a grin as he took a large gulp of the spiked drink. "Been waiting for that first sip all morning," said the fallen angel, smacking his lips.

Aaron sat at the edge of the office chair and began to stroke Gabriel's head.

"Does he seem smarter?" Zeke repeated, and then stifled a belch with his hand. "Yeah, I guess so, but what did you expect? You fixed him, you made him better—probably better than he ever was."

The angel took another drink.

Aaron sat back in his chair, soft-drink can between his legs, and shook his head in disbelief. "It's all a blur; I have no idea what I did."

Gabriel lay down on his side and closed his eyes. The room was silent except for the sound of the dog's rhythmic breathing as he quickly drifted off to sleep.

"What's happened to me, Zeke?" Aaron asked. There was fear in his voice and he struggled to maintain control. "What did that . . . animal thing inside my head do? Talk to me!"

Zeke's can of soda stopped midway to his mouth. "God's menagerie," he said. "Not animal thing. Let's try not to be disrespectful."

Aaron nodded. "Sorry," he said with a smirk.

"Most people see it as some kind of animal; a dove or a lion. All of His creations."

Zeke tipped the can of soda back and drained its contents. He then tossed the empty can into a trash bag beside the bed. "It made you complete," he said, answering Aaron's original question. "For the first time since you were born, you're how you're supposed to be."

"And how am I supposed to be?" Aaron asked, annoyed with the man's cryptic response.

"You're a Nephilim, Aaron, through and through."

Aaron slammed his fists down on the arms of the chair. "Stop calling me that!" he yelled angrily.

Gabriel jumped and lifted his head. *"Is everything okay?"* he asked.

"Sorry," Aaron apologized, and reached down to scratch beneath the dog's chin. "Everything's fine. You go back to sleep."

Gabriel lay back and almost immediately resumed his nap.

"Sorry to be the one to break it to you, but that's what you are," Zeke said. He had found another nip and was drinking the whiskey straight this time.

"So is this what your kind of angel does? What did you call yourself—a Gregory? Do Gregorys go around outing people who are Nephilim?"

Zeke chuckled and leaned his head back against the cracked plaster wall. "Grigori," he corrected. "And no, that's not what we do. Our assignment came directly from the Big Guy upstairs," he said, pointing to the ceiling. "And I don't mean Crazy Al in room five-twenty." He had some more whiskey before he continued. "God Himself told us what to do. Our job was a simple one really; it's amazing how badly we screwed it all up."

The fallen angel spoke slowly, remembering. "It was our job to keep an eye on mankind. They were still very young when we came here, and in need of guidance. We were to be their shepherds, you know, keep 'em out of trouble and all."

Zeke fell silent and a look of sadness darkened his features.

Aaron placed his empty soda can on the floor beside his chair. Someone in a room close by began to cough violently. "What happened?" he finally asked.

Zeke was staring at the small brown bottle in his hand and did not look up as he took a deep breath and continued. "We became a little too enamored with the locals, lost that professional distance." He nervously turned the bottle in his hand. "We began to teach them things, things the Lord felt they didn't need to know: how to make weapons, astrology, how to read the weather."

Zeke laughed harshly. "One of us sick bastards even taught the women about makeup." The angel brought the nip halfway to his mouth.

"So if your girlfriend spends two hours putting her face on before you go out for the evening, you can blame us."

"I actually don't have a girlfriend," Aaron said sheepishly, immediately thinking of Vilma.

Zeke finished the last of his liquor, ignoring Aaron's comment. "And they taught us things as well: how to drink, smoke, have sex. We went native," he said as he squinted into the empty bottle. Annoyed that there was nothing left, he tossed it to the floor. "We began to live like humans, act like humans. Some of us even took wives."

"And is that how the first Nephilim were born?" Aaron asked.

The fallen angel nodded. "You catch on quick. Yep, the Grigori are to blame for that whole mess—but not entirely." Zeke stood up and sloughed off his coat, draping it over the foot of the bed. "We weren't the only angels to find the human ladies attractive. There were others, deserters from the Great War in Heaven. They came to Earth to hide."

A Great War in Heaven; Aaron recalled the subject from John Milton's *Paradise Lost*. He'd read it in Mr. O'Leary's sophomore English class. "So that wasn't fiction?" he asked the Grigori. "There really was a war between angels?"

Zeke plopped himself back down on the bed. Aaron noticed a cigarette in one of his hands.

"It was real all right," Zeke answered.

He pinched the end of the cigarette between two fingers and tightly squeezed shut his eyes. Suddenly Aaron saw a flame and smoke. Zeke had lit the cigarette with his fingers. *I'm dreaming,* he thought.

"The Grigori weren't there for it, but from what I hear, it was pretty awful." The old angel took a drag and held it. He tilted his head back and blew the smoke into the air above him to form a billowing gray cloud.

"Not supposed to smoke in here either," he said, "but I can't help it. A real bitch to quit."

He took another puff and let it flow from his nostrils. "The Morningstar really blew it," Zeke said, returning to times past. "He didn't know how good he had it."

Aaron was confused. "The Morningstar?"

Zeke puffed greedily on the cigarette as if it were the last one he would ever have. "Lucifer. Lucifer Morningstar? Was once the right hand of God then got greedy? He and those who followed his lead screwed up even bigger than we did."

The room stank of smoke and Aaron wished there were a window to open. He waved his hand in front of his face in an attempt to breathe untainted air.

"Compared to what happened to him, we got off easy."

Gabriel started to dream as he lay on the floor; his legs twitched and paddled as if he were chasing something. Aaron grinned, distracted by his dog's antics. He had always been curious about his dreams. He'd have to ask Gabriel about it when he awoke.

He turned his attention back to Zeke. "You were punished?"

Zeke nodded ever so slowly, his eyes gazing off into the past as he remembered. "We were banished to Earth, never to see Heaven again. We wanted to be human so badly, we could live among them forever, they said." He sucked the cigarette down to the filter trying to get every last bit of carcinogen into his body.

"That wasn't so bad—was it?" Aaron asked, caution in his voice.

Zeke rubbed the tip of the cigarette's filter dead against the bedframe and flicked it to the floor. "Nah," he said in a dismissive tone. "Not really. It was what we wanted anyway."

Aaron could sense the angel's growing unrest. Zeke reached behind himself and began to rub the back of his neck and shoulder blades.

"Except they took our wings," he said. There was a tremble in his voice.

"Who . . . who took your wings?" Aaron asked.

"Who do you think?" Zeke answered sharply as he continued to rub his back and shoulders. "The Powers. They cut off our wings and . . . and they killed our children."

Zeke quickly swabbed at his eyes, smearing away any trace of emotion. Aaron wondered how long it had been since the angel had spoken of his past.

"They're ruthless, Aaron," he said. "They can sense when a Nephilim is reaching maturity—sometimes before. They hunt it down and kill it before it can gain full use of its birthright. That's why I did what I did—to give you a fighting chance."

Gabriel came suddenly awake as if sensing the pervasive atmosphere of sadness that now seemed to fill the tiny room with the cigarette smoke.

"*What is wrong?*" the dog asked, looking from Aaron to Zeke.

"Is that how you get even?" Aaron asked. "When you find us, you do something to turn us completely into Nephilim? Is that how you get back at the Powers for what they took from you?"

Zeke sadly shook his head. "I learned long ago not to interfere."

"And those others you've encountered—the Powers killed them?"

"Probably," Zeke said in a whisper. "Eventually."

"Why me then?" Aaron asked the fallen angel. "Why did you do it for me and not the others?"

Zeke shrugged. "I really don't know," he answered. "Something told me you're special."

chapter six

Inside the V.I. Lenin nuclear power plant, twenty-five kilometers upstream from the Ukraine city of Chernobyl, an angel screamed in rage.

Verchiel flung open two reinforced steel doors in the dilapidated structure that housed the number four reactor, the one that had exploded in 1986 rendering much of the surrounding Ukrainian countryside uninhabitable. In his time stationed upon this world, he had borne witness to the destructive potential of the human animal many times over, and wondered with disgust how long it would be before they destroyed themselves once and for all.

The master of the Powers strode into the reactor room, followed closely by six of his elite soldiers and the wild-eyed feral child held in check with collar and leash. The child coughed and sneezed as clouds of thick radioactive dust, undisturbed since the plant officially closed just a few years before, billowed into the air with their passing.

The explosion here had released forty times the amount of radioactivity unleashed by the atomic bombs dropped on Hiroshima and Nagasaki. Even now radiation levels were still incredibly high and quite dangerous to all forms of life. But that was of little concern to the nuclear power plant's current residents—or its visitors.

Verchiel stopped and stared with displeasure. The vast chamber had been turned into a place of worship, a makeshift church. An altar of sorts was laid out before him. Hundreds of candles of various sizes burned in front of a crude painting depicting an angelic being in the loving embrace of a mortal woman. And hovering in the sky above this coupling was an infant, a child glowing like the sun. Four figures, dressed in heavy woolen robes, knelt before the altar in silent prayer. Priests of the profane beliefs. They showed no sign that they were aware of his presence.

"Sacrilege!" Verchiel bellowed, his booming voice echoing off the concrete-and-metal walls of the high-ceilinged reactor chamber.

One of the figures stirred from his benediction, muttered something beneath his breath, and bowed his head to the shrine before he stood. The others continued their silent worship.

"Welcome to our holy place," he said.

"You disappoint me, Byleth," Verchiel responded as the figure at the crude altar gradually turned to face him. "A deserter and a disgrace to your host, but this . . ." He gestured to the shrine. "It offends the Almighty to the core of His Being."

Byleth smiled piously and strolled closer, hands clasped before him. "Does it really, Verchiel? Does the belief in a prophecy that preaches the reuniting of God with His fallen children really offend Him?" The robed angel stopped before them. "Or does it simply offend *you*?" Again Byleth smiled.

"What happened to you, Byleth?" Verchiel asked. "You were one of my finest soldiers. What made you fall so far from His grace?"

The angel chuckled softly as his hands disappeared inside the sleeves of his robe. "Is this usually what you ask before you kill us?"

Verchiel's lip curled back in a sneer. "It is merely an attempt to understand how you could turn your back upon a sacred duty to the Creator of all things."

"You must know these things before you condemn us to death?" Byleth asked, his gaze unwavering.

"Yes, before you are executed for your crimes," the Powers' commander answered. "A chance to purge yourself of guilt before the inevitable."

"I see," the priest said thoughtfully. "Has

Camael answered for his crimes?"

Verchiel was silent, an explosive rage building inside him.

The priest smiled, pleased with the lack of response. "That is good," Byleth said. "As long as he lives, there's a chance that—"

"It is only a matter of time before the traitor meets with his much deserved fate," Verchiel interrupted, his words dripping with malice.

"Did you feel it, Verchiel?" the angel asked, one of his hands leaving the confines of his robe to gently touch his forehead. "Just a few glorious hours ago, did you feel it come into its own?"

"I felt nothing," Verchiel lied. He had been en route to Ukraine when he felt the psychic disturbance. The angel had been tracking half-breeds for hundreds of thousands of years and never had he felt an emergence so strong. It concerned him. "And if I had, what more could it be but the manifestation of another blemish upon the Creator's world? Something to hunt down and eradicate before it has the opportunity to offend any further."

The boy began to cough and Byleth sadly gazed at the human child who struggled against the confines of his leash.

"That poor creature should never have been brought here, Verchiel," the angel priest said. "The poisons in this air will do it irreparable harm."

Verchiel gazed at the creature with complete

disinterest and looked back to the priest. "How else was I to find you in a timely manner?" he asked. "If it should die then so be it; I'll find another monkey to help with my hunt."

The others at the altar were standing now and had turned to watch the encounter. They all wore the same idiotic grin and Verchiel could not wait to see it burned from their faces.

"There is desperation in your tone, Verchiel. You felt it as strongly as we," Byleth said as he shared a moment with his fellow worshippers. "And you are afraid—afraid that the prophecy is coming to fruition."

Verchiel snarled and spread his wings, knocking Byleth to the floor by the altar in a cloud of radioactive dust. "What black sorcery did the human seer use to corrupt so many of you? Tell me so I might have any who practice such poisonous villainy scoured from the planet."

"Always so dramatic, Verchiel," Byleth said, struggling to his feet. "There was no magic, no corrupting spell. Nothing but a vision of unification and an end to the violence."

A sword of fire grew in Verchiel's hand. The larger particles of irradiated dust and dirt in the air sparked as they drifted into contact with the divine flame. Following his lead, his soldiers each manifested blazing weapons as well.

"And what has this idyllic vision brought you thus far?" asked the Powers' leader. "You hide yourself away in the poisoned wastelands created by the animals, denying your true place in the order of things. Is this some kind of punishment, Byleth? Do you think that this half-breed prophet you imagine is coming will look upon you fondly because of it?" Verchiel said with disgust. "Pathetic."

"This place and the poisoned land around it reminds us of what we were and what we have become," Byleth explained. "Once, we were filled with His holy virtue, on a mission to wipe away evil—but we were tainted by the violence and a self-righteousness that said we were acting in His name."

"Everything I do, I do for Him," Verchiel replied, his fiery blade burning brighter and radiating an intense heat.

"That is what you believe to be true," Byleth said. "But there is another way—a way without death, a way that brings the end of our exile and the beginning of our redemption." The angel held out his hand, directing Verchiel to look upon the altar. "*This* is the way, Verchiel. *This* is our future."

Verchiel shook his head. "No, it is blasphemy." He raised a hand to his soldiers behind him. "Remove them from the altar," he commanded.

The Powers leaped into the air, their wings stirring choking clouds of fine, radioactive debris.

"We will fight you, Verchiel!" Byleth cried. A weapon of fire grew in his grip, and others blazed up in the hands of his fellow believers, yet they seemed pitiful by comparison to the swords of the Powers. Feeble wings grew from their backs.

"Look at you," Verchiel said as he strode toward them and their sacred shrine. "Belief in this heresy has reduced you to mere shadows of your former glory. How sad."

"Our past sins have made us thus," Byleth bellowed in anger as he leaped at Verchiel, his sword held high.

But he was intercepted by the savagery of Verchiel's elite guard and forced to the ground beneath their weight. Verchiel watched with great amusement as the priests were hauled away from their shrine.

"This is the future, you say?" he asked as he looked from them to the burning candles and crude artwork.

They struggled against their captors, but the Powers' soldiers held them fast. "It won't end with us," Byleth hissed. "That which has been foretold now walks among us."

Verchiel looked to the altar, fiery indignation burning in his breast. "I see no future here," he said as he flapped his powerful wings. The mighty gusts of air extinguished the candles and toppled the offensive painting. "All I see is the end."

Verchiel grinned maliciously as he turned back to the priests, but his triumph quickly turned to confusion when he noted the serene looks upon their faces.

"It's far from over, Verchiel," Byleth said.

"Look for yourself," he added with a tilt of his head toward the altar.

The Powers' leader turned and watched with horror as the candles, one by one, began to re-ignite. In a burst of fury, he spread his wings and launched himself toward the grinning priest, once a soldier in his service. Savagely he thrust the end of his fiery blade into Byleth's chest, reveling in the change of his expression from a grin of the enlightened to one of excruciating pain.

Byleth's fellow priests gasped in unison. "Please," one of his fellow believers plaintively whispered.

Verchiel leaned in close, watching the flesh of the renegade angel's face bubble and blacken as he burned from within. "They beg for mercy, but alas, their words fall upon deaf ears."

Byleth slid to the floor, Verchiel's blade still within him, his heavy robes beginning to ignite. "And . . . and how are *your* words received, Verchiel?" He gasped as he lifted his head, puddles of liquid flesh sizzling upon the dust-covered ground. "What does the Lord of Lords have to say when *you* speak?"

Verchiel pulled his sword from the priest's chest. "The Almighty and I . . . we do not need to converse."

Byleth smiled hideously, his teeth nothing more than charred nubs protruding from oozing black gums. "As I imagined."

Verchiel felt his ire rise. "That amuses you,

Byleth? My lack of communication with the Heavenly Father makes you smile in the face of your imminent death?"

His body awash in flames, the priest slowly raised his charred, skeletal hands to the sides of his face—to where his ears used to be. "Deaf . . . ears," Byleth whispered. "Deaf ears." And then he began to laugh.

The sound enraged Verchiel. He pulled back his arm and brought the heavenly blade down upon the burning priest once, twice, three times, reducing his offender to ash. Then he turned from the smoking remains to face his prisoners. "This is what the profanity of your beliefs has brought you," he said, directing their attention to the ruin of their master.

The sword of flame receded to nothing, and Verchiel strode away toward the doors that would take him from the poisonous chamber.

"Kill them," he said, void of emotion, his back to them. "I want to forget they ever existed."

And he left the room, the screams of the dying priests escorting him on his journey, the malignant words of an ancient prophecy feverishly swirling around in his mind.

Michael Jonas glanced at his watch. He set his pen down on top of the insurance forms he was in the process of completing and picked up the phone.

Where is he? the psychiatrist wondered.

The dial tone droned in his ear as he searched for Aaron's phone number in his file. He punched in the numbers and listened as it began to ring.

Aaron Corbet had been nothing but punctual all the years that he'd treated him, and Jonas found it odd that he would simply blow off their appointment, especially after their discussion yesterday morning.

He would have been lying if he had said he wasn't fascinated by the rather unique talent the young man had exhibited; in all his twenty-five years of practicing he'd never seen anything quite so bizarre and yet, exciting. Certainly Aaron could be delusional, and was already fluent in Portuguese, Spanish, and Latin, but his gut told him no. Jonas grew eager with the thought of the papers he might publish on this specific case, and the accolades he would receive from his peers.

"Hello?" answered a woman's voice from the other end of the line.

"Yes, hi," Jonas said in greeting. "Is Aaron there please?"

"No, he's not," the woman replied. "Can I ask who's calling?"

He would need to be cautious; patient-doctor confidentiality was an issue. "This is Michael Jonas," he responded professionally. "Is this Mrs. Stanley?"

"Yes, Dr. Jonas. How are you? Aaron went out with the dog early this morning and he hasn't returned." There was a pause and Jonas knew what was coming next. After being a psychiatrist for so many years he could read people and their reactions. "Is there a problem, Doctor? Is . . . is Aaron going to see you again?"

She was concerned and he wanted to put her mind at ease without sharing Aaron's personal business.

"No need for panic, Mrs. Stanley. I'm just checking in, calling to see how he's doing. Would you have him get in touch with me when he comes in? I should be at the office until well after six."

"Certainly, Doctor," she said, less tension in her tone. "I'll give him the message."

"Thanks so much, Mrs. Stanley. You have a good day."

"Same to you," she responded, and hung up.

Jonas returned the receiver to the cradle and again glanced at his watch. *Interesting,* he thought. *Aaron went out early and no one's seen him since.* Jonas wondered if he had frightened him away. Maybe he shouldn't have mentioned his friend at Mass General.

The cartoon image of a scholarly paper with flapping wings flying out a window danced across his mind and he smiled. Jonas reached for his pen to resume his weekly paperwork and saw that he wasn't alone.

"Jesus Christ!" he gasped as he threw himself back against his chair, startled.

A man stood in front of his desk. He appeared older, but was tall, striking, and although he wore a suit, Jonas could see that he was in good physical condition.

"How did you get in here?" Jonas asked nervously.

The man simply stood staring at the desktop. He seemed to be studying Jonas's paperwork.

"Can I help you with something, Mr. . . . ?"

The stranger said nothing, continuing to gaze at the top of the desk. And then he raised his head and looked at Jonas. He was handsome in a distinguished kind of way. He reminded the psychiatrist of the actor who used to play James Bond, and later starred in that movie about the Russian submarine. But it was his eyes that were strangely different. There was something wrong with them. Jonas thought of the eyes of a stuffed owl that his grandmother had kept on display at her summer cottage in Maine: dark black in the center and encircled with gold.

"Camael," the stranger answered in a powerful timbre. "I am Camael—and I've come in search of the child."

Camael tilted his head back and sniffed the air. "The child was here," he said as he turned in a slow circle, "not long ago—a day perhaps." He moved closer to the desk, the sour smell of the human's fear mixing with the strong essence of the Nephilim. It was a masculine odor, a male scent. "I mean the child no harm, but it is imperative that I find him."

Dr. Jonas stood and slammed his meaty hands down onto the desktop aggressively. "Listen," he said, "I don't have a clue as to what you're talking about."

The psychiatrist was a large man. He might have been powerful once, but the years had been unkind and his body had gone to seed. He pointed a square finger authoritatively to the door. "So I'm going to have to ask you to leave."

As if on cue, the office door swung slowly open and Camael snarled as two of Verchiel's Powers came into the room.

The two took notice of him immediately and emitted a snakelike hiss from their mouths. "The betrayer," spat one with a head of jet-black hair, his body lowering to a readied crouch. It had been millennia since Camael had last commanded them, but he believed this one was called Hadriel.

"What the hell is going on here?" the human blustered. "Leave my office at once or I'm going to . . ."

"Silence, ape!" the other angel warned. Camael knew the name of this one for certain. He was Cassiel, one of Verchiel's crueler operatives.

"I strongly advise you to take cover, Doctor," Camael warned. He did not take his eyes from the Powers, feeling that special calm before battle slowly wash over him.

"This *ape* is going to call the police," the

flustered psychiatrist said as he reached for the telephone on his desk.

Cassiel moved as a blur. His hand shot out and from his fingertips a searing white light emanated. "I asked you to be quiet."

The doctor screamed out in agony as his body burst into flame. He fell back against the wall and crumpled to the floor, completely engulfed by fire. He twitched and thrashed in excruciating death and everywhere he touched began to burn as well.

Camael used the distraction to strike. In his mind he saw the weapon he wanted and it formed in his grasp, composed of heavenly fire. He attacked, swinging the burning blade at Hadriel, who seemed engrossed in the psychiatrist's death throes. But the angel reacted quickly, summoning a weapon of his own, a spear—and blocking the swipe that would have certainly taken his head.

The weapons clashed, sounding like the grumble of thunder.

"The great Camael," Hadriel taunted as he pushed him away and thrust forward with the burning spear. "One of our greatest, reduced to living amongst the human animals."

Camael sidestepped to avoid the spear thrust and brought his blade down, cutting his attacker's weapon explosively in two. "You talk too much, Hadriel," he said as he stepped in close and lashed out, the pommel of the sword connecting with the side of the soldier's head, bringing him to his knees. "A human trait, I believe," Camael said to the stunned angel.

Camael heard the whisper of another weapon cutting through the air. He unfurled his wings and flew upward as Cassiel's sword passed harmlessly beneath him.

"Are you lonely, Camael?" Cassiel asked as he too pushed off from the floor and spread his wings to join him in the air.

Camael parried Cassiel's next thrust and maneuvered in closer. He brought a knee up sharply into the angel's stomach. "My mission is all the company I need," he said as he drove his forehead into the angel's face. "I've grown to enjoy my solitude."

Cassiel plummeted to the floor.

The office was on fire and a thick black smoke filled the air.

"Despised by your brothers, feared by the kind you once destroyed." Cassiel struggled to all fours. He looked up at Camael and smiled. "All for the ramblings of an animal plagued by madness."

"Feel no sadness for me, brother," Camael said as he glided down toward the angel, his sword at the ready. "But ask yourself this: What if the seer was right? What if it all turns out to be true? What then?"

Cassiel shrieked and attacked again. "It will never come to be," he screamed as a dagger appeared in his hand and he slashed at Camael, driving him away. "Lies, all lies!"

Camael recoiled from a swipe of Cassiel's blade, reared back, and drove the heel of his foot into the angel's chest. Cassiel was propelled back by the force of the blow and tumbled over a chair in front of the desk.

The smoke had grown thicker and Camael knew that it wouldn't be long before the office was completely consumed by fire. He had to find out the identity of the boy. *The essence about this Nephilim is strong, perhaps the strongest I have ever felt,* he thought. *So strong, in fact, that the Powers had no need of a tracker to find him.* He tensed, waiting for Cassiel to rise, his mind aflutter. *Could he be the reason why Verchiel has increased the frequency and savagery of his attacks?* He again dared to wonder, *could this actually be the One?*

Camael screamed out in sudden pain and rage as Hadriel's spear tore through his shoulder from behind. It was sloppy of him. Distracted by his musings, he had failed to notice Verchiel's other henchman emerge from the thick smoke, a new weapon in hand.

"Finish him," Cassiel ordered as he climbed to his feet among the flames.

Hadriel pulled back the spearhead and lunged again, but this time Camael was ready. He sprang from the floor, wings spread. He had summoned new weapons as well—short swords—from the armory of his imagination and held one firmly in each hand.

Hadriel's thrust passed beneath him and before he could react, Camael brought one of his swords viciously down, cleaving the angel's skull like the wood of a rotted tree stump.

"No!" Cassiel shrieked as he soared toward Camael, eager to avenge his fallen comrade.

"Verchiel's soldiers have grown sloppy," Camael taunted as he pulled the weapon from the angel's skull and blocked the enraged Cassiel's attack with it. He thrust upward with the other blade and pierced his attacker's chest.

Cassiel wailed and thrashed, his wings beating frantically, as he fell to the floor clutching at the weeping chest wound.

Camael strode through the smoke and fire toward his fallen foe. "What does Verchiel know about this one—the Nephilim boy?" he questioned. "Tell me and I'll let you live."

Cassiel struggled to his feet using the wall for support. "You'll let me live? Do you hear yourself, Camael? I thought you deserted the Powers because you tired of the violence, of all the killing." The angel held a trembling hand to his bleeding wound. "I think you've become what you most hate," Cassiel hissed as he reached into the fire by the wall and pulled out the blackened, still-burning skull of the psychiatrist and hurled it at him.

Camael hacked at the flaming projectile,

cutting it in two as it neared him. Using the moment, Cassiel spread his wings and leaped toward the burning curtains across the room. The fleeing angel passed through the flaming material, and then the glass of the window beyond, to escape with an explosive crash.

The fire burned brighter, larger, as the sudden blast of oxygen fed the hungry conflagration.

The Nephilim's identity more important than pursuit, Camael rushed to the desk. The papers strewn about its surface had already started to smolder and curl. His eyes scanned the documents, searching for something—anything that would tell him who the boy was.

Beneath a folder charred at the edges, he saw it. A single sentence scrawled upon a piece of notepaper attached to a file. "Patient believes he now has the ability to understand and speak all foreign languages."

Camael snatched up the folder. Something moaned above him and he moved out of the way as a portion of the ceiling collapsed in a shower of flaming debris. In the distance, the mournful howls of fire engines filled the air. He had what he needed and prepared to leave the scene with haste.

Time was of the essence, for as soon as Verchiel learned of his involvement, all Hell would most assuredly break loose.

chapter seven

Within the unused bell tower of the Church of the Blessed Sacrament, Verchiel stared into the familiar face of human mortality. Since the Powers' return from the poisonous wasteland that was Chernobyl, their human tracker had fallen terribly ill. The poor creature lay upon a plastic tarp in a darkened area of the tower where once a bell had hung. It shivered, moaning softly as it slowly died from the radioactive poisons it had been exposed to on their last hunt.

"Is there nothing more you can do for it?" Verchiel asked the human healer who was administering to the wounded Cassiel.

The healer, called Kraus, turned his blind, cataract-covered eyes toward the sound of Verchiel's voice.

"I've done all I can, my master," he said as he nimbly plucked a golden needle from inside a worn leather satchel and deftly placed a thick thread through its eye. His lack of vision had not affected his skill with a needle. "It won't be long before he succumbs to—"

"Its skill served me well," the Powers' leader interrupted, taking his eyes from the dying boy covered in black oozing sores. "It will be bothersome to find another."

Verchiel moved across the cluttered tower, its space now used for storage, to loom over the healer and his current patient, the boy almost completely forgotten. "And you, Cassiel," he asked smoothly, "have you served me as well?"

"Yes, my lord," Cassiel answered breathlessly as he lay upon the dusty floor while the blind old man sewed closed his wound.

"You say that Camael was there before you?" Verchiel asked as he watched the old man, whose job it was to care for the angels' physical forms, pull shut the wound in his soldier's chest with skillful stitches. Though primitive by angelic standards, the human apes did occasionally surprise even him with their usefulness.

Verchiel squatted beside the healer as he completed the task. "He will heal?" Verchiel asked. "The wound will not kill him?"

Kraus flinched from the power of Verchiel's voice. "It . . . it will not," the man stammered as he turned his blind gaze toward his master. "The injury will need time to mend, but it will heal."

What is it about the defective ones, the blind, the

mentally challenged, that makes them such superior servants? Verchiel wondered, thinking of the nonimpaired humans often driven to madness just by being in the angels' presence.

"You are done here," Verchiel proclaimed, and gently brushed the top of the older man's head with the tips of his fingers. "See to the tracker; ease him into death if need be."

The man gasped aloud, his body trembling as if in rapture, as if touched by God—or the next best thing. Kraus folded shut his satchel of healing instruments and scurried away to the darkened corner to help a dying member of his own breed.

Perhaps their imperfections make them more receptive to the extraordinary. It was a hypothesis Verchiel hoped to explore further someday, when their mission was finally complete. He roused himself from his contemplation. There was still much to do.

"The Nephilim I sense so keenly—what information have you brought of him?" Verchiel asked Cassiel, who still lay upon the wooden floor.

"I bring information about Camael," Cassiel said eagerly. "Living amongst the apes has made him frail and weak. It . . . it can only be a matter of time before we destroy the traitor and . . ."

"Frail and weak, you say?" Verchiel asked, a sour smile upon his thin lips. In the church below, Mass was beginning with the sound of a pipe organ. The melodious chords of a hymn drifted up into the bell tower. The music annoyed him. "But not so frail and weak as to prevent him from slaying Hadriel and gravely wounding you?"

Cassiel squirmed, struggling to sit up. "The . . . the space was cramped and there was blinding smoke. Please . . ."

The music from the church below came to an end and the murmuring of prayer began.

"So you bring me nothing of the half-breed?"

Cassiel pushed himself into a sitting position. A dark fluid began to seep from around the wound's stitching as his movements pulled them taut. "The fire . . . it was burning out of control and Camael was already present. There was little we could do . . ."

The piteous words of his soldier enraged Verchiel almost as much as the monkeys' attempts to speak with God drifting up from the ceremony in the church below. Verchiel reached down to Cassiel's wound and dug his fingers beneath the stitching.

Cassiel screamed.

"Silence," Verchiel spat as he tore the thick, black thread away from the angel's flesh.

How dare they think they can speak to Him, he thought, revolted by the worshippers praying in the church below. *If the Lord God will not speak with me, then why do they have the audacity to believe that He would listen to* their *pathetic chatter?*

Verchiel thought, perturbed. He cast aside the surgical thread and bits of torn skin that dangled from it.

Cassiel lay silently writhing upon the floor, his wound now gaping wide, and weeping.

"You failed me," Verchiel growled as he picked Cassiel up from the floor and held him aloft. "And I do not deal well with failure."

The organ played again and the monkeys were singing. *Why do they insist on doing that?* he wondered. Did they believe that the discordant sounds from their primitive mouths would please the Creator, He who had orchestrated the *symphony* of creation?

Cassiel flapped his wings as he struggled in his leader's grasp. "Master Verchiel . . . mercy," he wheezed.

Verchiel needed to hear something other than the animals' wailing below, something that would calm his frenzied state. Holding Cassiel by the throat, he reached out and grabbed one of his soldier's wings.

"Please . . . no," Cassiel pleaded.

Verchiel took the delicate appendage in his hand and began to bend it, to twist it. The sound was horrible—sharp—as the cartilage gave way beneath his grip. The angel was screaming, begging and crying to be forgiven for his trespasses.

Verchiel let Cassiel drop from his hands. The angel sobbed, his wing twisted at an obscene angle.

"Administer to him," Verchiel barked, knowing that the healer was listening from the shadows, waiting to serve. "Disappoint me again, and I'll tear them both from your body," Verchiel instructed Cassiel as he turned his back upon him.

He had decided to be merciful; it was what the Creator would have done.

Aaron was dreaming again.

An old man with a milky white eye is using a pointed stick to write on a tablet made of red clay.

Aaron looks around at his surroundings. Where the hell am I? he wonders. He is in a single-room structure, a hut, and it appears to be made out of straw and large mud bricks. Primitive oil lamps placed around the room provide the only source of light. It stinks of body odor and urine.

The old man is deathly thin, his hair and beard incredibly long. There are things living in the wild expanse of his hair. He finishes a symbol on the clay tablet and slowly raises his shaggy head to Aaron.

He points the writing instrument and in a guttural tongue he speaks. "It is you I see in the future—you I write of now."

The bad eye rolls obscenely in the right socket, and Aaron cannot help but think of the moon.

The old man reaches down with a skeletal hand covered in a thin, almost translucent layer of spotted skin and turns the tablet so Aaron can see—so he can read.

Gazing down at the primitive script, Aaron knows what the man has written. It is a prediction of some kind, something about the union of angel and mortal woman, creating a bridge for those who have fallen.

What the heck does that mean? he wonders. He starts to speak but stops, interrupted by screams from outside the hovel, and something else.

The old man stares at him and slowly brings a hand up to cover the bad eye. "Go now," he whispers. "You have seen your destiny. Now you must fulfill it."

Cries of fear are moving closer, and there is another sound in the air—a now familiar sound that fills him with dread.

The pounding sound of wings.

Aaron came awake with a choking gasp. His heart raced and his body crawled with nervous perspiration.

He could still hear wings flapping, and then they were silent.

Gabriel, lying beside him atop the covers, had also awakened and was staring at him.

"Did I wake you, boy?" Aaron asked groggily as he reached out from under the bedclothes and stroked the dog's head. "Sorry, bad dreams again."

As he patted the dog he felt himself begin to calm, his pulse rate slow. Gabriel was as good as a tranquilizer.

The dog licked his hand affectionately. *"The*

old man was scary, wasn't he?" Gabriel said, nuzzling closer.

"Old man? You mean Zeke, Gabe?" Aaron asked, eyes beginning to close, still patting the velvety fur that covered the dog's hard head.

The dog turned his gaze to him. *"No, not Zeke,"* he answered, *"the old man in the dream. He scared me, too."*

It hit him with the force of a pile driver. Aaron struggled beneath the sheets and blanket into a sitting position. He reached over and turned on the bedside light.

"How do you know about the old man in the dream, Gabriel?" Aaron asked, terrified by what the answer might be.

"I dreamed it," the dog answered proudly. His tail thumped happily. *"I have different dreams now, not just running and jumping and chasing rabbits."*

Aaron leaned back and let his head bounce off the wooden headboard. "I can't believe this. You had the same dream as I did?"

"Yes," Gabriel said. *"Why did his eye look like the moon, Aaron?"*

Aaron felt as though he were on a roller coaster, perpetually plunging farther and farther into darkness, picking up speed, with no sign of the horrific ride's end.

And there was nothing he wanted more than to get off.

"Please make it stop," he whispered.

Gabriel crawled closer and lay his chin upon

Aaron's leg. *"It's all right, Aaron,"* the dog said devotedly. *"Don't be sad."*

Aaron opened his eyes and began to pat the dog again. "It's not all right, Gabe. Everything is spinning out of control. What's happening to me—what's happened to you, it . . . isn't right."

Gabriel pushed himself into a sitting position and pressed his butt against his master. *"I was hurt very badly and you made me better,"* the dog said with a tilt of his head. *"Are you upset that I'm . . . different now?"*

Aaron looked his best friend in the eyes and shook his head. "No, I'm not upset about that. Matter of fact, that's the only thing about this business that I'm willing to get used to." He reached out and stroked the side of the dog's head. "It's everything else—the bizarro dreams, the stuff Zeke's been telling me. . . ."

He leaned back against the headboard again and sighed with exasperation. "I don't want this, Gabriel. I have enough to worry about. I have to finish high school with a decent enough GPA to get into a good college."

"GPA?" the dog questioned. *"What is this GPA?"*

"Grade point average," Aaron explained. "Doing very, very well in my classes at school."

Gabriel nodded in understanding.

"All this crap about angels and Nephilim—I don't care if it's true, I just can't deal with it." At that moment Aaron made a decision. "I'm gonna tell Zeke I'm done. I don't want to know anything else. Everything is going to be just like it was before my birthday."

He glanced at the clock on the nightstand. It was close to four A.M. and he wanted to go back to sleep; he was both mentally and physically exhausted. But he also feared the dreams.

"Well, let's give this another try," he said as he reached over and switched off the light. He lay his head down on the pillow and put his arm around the dog.

"Good night, Aaron," Gabriel said as he moved up to share the pillow. *"Try and dream only good dreams."*

"I'll do my best, pal," Aaron answered, and before long, fell into a deep sleep active with dreams, not of old men, ancient prophecies, and angels, but of running very fast in the sunshine and chasing rabbits.

Verchiel noiselessly descended the winding wooden steps from the bell tower of the Blessed Sacrament Church. The stairway was enshrouded in total darkness, but it meant nothing to a being that had navigated the void before the Almighty brought about the light of Creation.

At the foot of the stairs was a locked door, and Verchiel willed the simple mechanism to open, and it swung wide to admit him to the place of worship. The angel found his way from the back room where the holy men prepared themselves to address their tribe, and went out onto the altar. He gazed above him at the steepled ceiling and the giant cross of gold, the symbol of their faith, hanging there. From his place on the altar, he looked out at the church, the early morning sunrise diluted by colorful stained glass windows. There was a certain peacefulness here that he did not expect from the animals.

Verchiel stepped from the altar and strode down the aisle. When he had traveled half the length of the church, he turned to face the great hanging cross. This was how the primitives did it, he mused, taking in the sight before him. This was how they attempted to communicate with God.

He recalled the countless times that he scoffed at their crude practices, as they built their altars of stone and wood and attempted to speak to the one true God through the act of prayer. It was a thought that filled him with unease, but perhaps this house of worship was where he could re-establish his connection with Heaven and again converse with the Creator of all things.

He recalled how they did it—how they prayed—and moved into one of the wooden pews. Awkwardly Verchiel knelt down and folded his hands before him, his dark eyes upon the altar ahead.

"It is I, Lord," he uttered in the language of animals. "It has been too long since we last spoke, and I am in need of Your guidance."

The angel gazed around the holy place for signs that he was being heard. There was nothing but the fading echo of his own voice.

Perhaps if he were closer. He left the pew and strode back to the altar.

"My mission, my very reason for existence, grows murky these days."

He gazed intently at the golden cross, hanging in the air above.

"There is a prophecy of which I'm certain You are aware. It talks about forgiveness and mercy for those who have fallen from Your grace, oh Heavenly Father."

Verchiel began to pace in front of the altar.

"It says that You will forgive them their most horrid trespasses—and that there will be a prophet of sorts, one who will act as the bringer of absolution."

He was growing agitated, angry. The air around him crackled with suppressed hostility. "And he will be a Nephilim," Verchiel spat, reviled by the word. "A Nephilim, a creature unfit to live beneath Your gaze, a mockery of life that I have done my best to eradicate from Your world with fire and flood."

The angel stopped pacing. "The wicked say that the time for the prophecy is nigh, that soon a bridge between the fallen angels and Heaven will be established." He moved up onto the altar, his gaze never wavering from the golden symbol. "You need to tell me, Lord. Do I follow my instincts and ignore the blasphemous writings of those little better than monkeys? Or do I ignore the purpose bestowed upon me after the Great War in Heaven? I need to know, my Father. Do I continue with my sacred chores and destroy all that offends You, or should I step back and let the prophecy prevail?"

Verchiel waited, expecting some kind of sign, but there was none, his plaintive questions met with silence.

The rage that had served him in war all these many millennia exploded from inside him. His wings came forth from his back and a mighty blade of flame appeared in his grasp. He shook the burning sword at the cross and voiced his anger. "Tell me, my God, for I am lost. Give me some indication of Your will."

There was a sound from somewhere upon the altar, and Verchiel stood mesmerized.

Has the Creator heard my plea? the angel thought. Was the Almighty about to bestow upon him a sign to assuage his doubts?

An old woman came out from the back room, a plastic bucket of water in one hand and a mop in the other. It was obvious that she had heard his supplication and was curious to see who prayed so powerfully.

Her eyes bulged from her ancient skull at the

sight of him. The bucket of soapy water slipped from her grasp to spill upon the altar floor.

What an awesome sight he must be to behold, he mused, spreading his wings to their full span, catching the muted, morning sunlight.

She attempted to flee, wild panic in her spastic movements, but stopped cold in her tracks. An ancient hand, skeletal with age, clutched frantically at her chest and her mouth opened in a silent howl. The old woman fell to the ground in a heap, her dying gaze rooted upon the golden symbol of her faith displayed above her.

Verchiel smiled. "So nice to hear from You again," he purred, divining meaning from what he had just borne witness to.

"Thy will be done."

Still in his sweatpants and T-shirt, Aaron slowly descended the stairs. Gabriel waited eagerly at the bottom. Aaron yawned and smacked his lips. The foul taste of sleep still coated the inside of his mouth. Hopefully he could get some juice and then get back upstairs to run a toothbrush around his mouth before he had to speak to anybody.

He'd slept longer than he wanted to, but seeing that he'd had some problems last night, and that it was Sunday, he wasn't all that concerned—just very thirsty.

"Can I eat now?" Gabriel asked from his side as Aaron padded barefoot down the hallway to the kitchen.

"Just as soon as I get some juice," he told the dog.

The linoleum was cold on the soles of his feet, and it helped to clear away the grogginess that came with morning. Lori sat at the table beneath the kitchen window, feeding cereal to Stevie.

"Hey," Aaron said, pulling on the refrigerator door.

"Hey, yourself," his mother answered.

Gabriel momentarily left his side to wish Lori and Stevie a good morning. Aaron almost drank from the carton, but thought better of it and reached to the cabinet for a glass. Filling it halfway, he leaned against the counter and attempted to quench his great thirst.

Lori was staring at him. She had that look on her face, the one that said something was wrong—that she had bad news to tell. Aaron was familiar with the look; it was the same one she'd worn when the family vacation to Disney World was canceled because the travel agency had unexpectedly gone out of business. They never did get to Disney.

"What's wrong?" he asked.

Stevie decided to feed himself and took the spoon from her. He shoveled a mound of Sugar Smacks onto the spoon and then, halfway to his mouth, dumped it on the floor.

Gabriel immediately went to work cleaning up the spillage.

"Stevie, no," Lori said as she took the spoon away from the child and pushed the bowl from his reach. "I have some really bad news for you," she said, placing a soiled, rolled-up napkin on the table.

"What is it?" Aaron asked, moving to join her.

Lynn's Sunday newspaper was on the table, and she turned it around so that he could see the headline.

PSYCHIATRIST KILLED IN BLAZE it read.

Aaron wasn't sure why he should be upset, until he noticed the picture that accompanied the story. The picture was of Lynn firefighters as they fought the blaze in an office building. The caption below read, "Dr. Michael Jonas was killed yesterday when his office at 257 Boston Street was engulfed in flames. Fire officials are still investigating the blaze, but believe that a gas leak may have been responsible for the explosion."

Aaron pried his eyes from the newspaper and looked at his mother. "Oh my God" was all he could manage.

Lori reached across the table and squeezed his hand. "I'm so sorry, hon," she said supportively. "Did you try to reach him last night?"

Aaron heard the question at the periphery of his thoughts. Dr. Jonas was dead. He was supposed to have seen the man yesterday, but after the business with Zeke, he'd completely forgotten. He'd planned on calling Monday to apologize.

His mother's hand was still on his. She gave it a squeeze. "Aaron?" she asked.

"I'm sorry," he said. "I zoned out. What did you say?"

"Dr. Jonas—he called yesterday while you were out," she answered. "Did you try to return his call?"

Aaron slowly shook his head. "He called? I . . . I didn't see the message."

When he'd come in last night he'd been tired. The family was out to supper, and the quiet in the house was so inviting. He'd fed Gabriel, taken him out, and then gone up to bed to watch some television. He hadn't even thought to check for messages.

"I didn't know he called," he said dreamily, picturing the man just two days ago, full of life and eager to help him. "How could this happen?" he asked, not expecting an answer.

"They said it was probably a gas leak," Lori replied as she picked up the child's cereal bowl and brought it to the sink.

Stevie got down from his chair and toddled off toward the family room, oblivious to anything in his path.

Gabriel hovered around Aaron and he realized that the dog had yet to be fed. "I'm sorry, pal," he said, going to the drainboard at the sink and retrieving the dog's food bowl.

Lori was doing the breakfast dishes. "If it was gas, just one spark would do the trick—"

Aaron filled Gabriel's bowl and placed it on the mat near his water dish. His mother was still talking, but it was her last words that created the disturbing image in his mind.

He saw Zeke lighting his cigarette.

"If it was gas . . ."

His mother's words echoed through his head.

Zeke lit his smoke with the tips of his fingers. Fire from the tips of his fingers.

". . . just one spark would do the trick."

chapter eight

Aaron couldn't wait for Monday to arrive.

Ken Curtis High had become his safe haven. Once behind its walls, the rules were simple—go to class, do the homework, take the test. Not so in the real world lately, a place that was becoming less and less real for him with each passing day.

At school he could push thoughts of talking dogs, Nephilim, Powers, and death to the back of his cluttered mind—at least until the bell rang at two thirty. School was the ultimate distraction, and that was exactly what he craved.

At lunchtime Aaron was at his locker dropping off books from his morning classes. He wasn't feeling hungry, but knowing he had to work at the clinic right after school, he figured he should probably eat something.

His psychology text slipped to the floor, and

his thoughts turned to Michael Jonas as he bent to pick it up. The questions flooded forward as if a faucet had been turned on to its maximum. *What really caused the fire?*

He saw Zeke's fingertip flash and his cigarette ignite.

Why am I thinking like this? he wondered, returning the book to the shelf in the locker. He knew that Zeke didn't have anything to do with the fire that took his psychiatrist's life. The newspaper said it had started in the early afternoon, when he and Gabriel had been with the fallen angel in his hotel room.

But what about the others? he thought with a wave of foreboding. *What about the . . . Powers?*

His stomach churned uneasily as he slammed closed his locker. *Maybe I'll just skip lunch and go to the library.*

Head down, he turned and nearly plowed into Vilma Santiago.

Aaron stumbled back. "Hi," he blurted out nervously. "Didn't see you there, sorry."

"Hi."

She seemed unconcerned with his clumsiness, but as nervous around him as he was feeling around her. In the background by her locker, he could see two of her friends playing Secret Weasel, trying not to be noticed.

"How're you doing?" Aaron asked lamely. If he hadn't blown it yet, it was only a matter of time.

"I'm good," she answered. "How're you?"

"I'm good," he said with a nervous nod and an idiot grin. "Real good." His mind was blank, completely void of all electrical activity. He had no idea what to say next, and wondered how she'd react if he started to cry.

The silence was becoming painfully awkward when she spoke. "Are you going to lunch?" she asked, looking quickly away.

And all of a sudden lunch seemed like a wonderful idea.

"Yeah, lunch is great—it's lunchtime—sure, I'm going to lunch." Aaron couldn't believe how he was acting. *What a complete idiot.* He wouldn't blame her in the least if she turned around and walked away. No. *Ran* away.

"Do you want to have lunch with me?" she asked, her voice growing incredibly soft, as if expecting rejection.

He was speechless. No words available, please try again later. He was horrified, he couldn't even think of something *stupid* to say.

Vilma suddenly looked embarrassed. "If you have something else to do, I completely understand and . . ."

"I'd love to," he finally managed. "Sorry . . . it's just that I'm kind of . . . y'know, surprised, that you'd want me to."

She smiled slyly, and it felt as though the temperature in the hallway rose sixty degrees. *Great, now I'm sweating,* he thought. *Real cool.*

"I'm full of surprises, Aaron Corbet," she said with a flip of her dark hair. "So, do you want to go to the caf or off campus?"

Just then somebody called his name. They both turned to see Mrs. Vistorino, the guidance office secretary, coming down the hallway. She was notorious for her brightly colored pantsuits, and today she was wearing lime green with shoes to match.

"Aaron," Mrs. Vistorino called again. "I'm glad I caught you."

"Is there something wrong?" he asked cautiously, the sickly feeling in the pit of his stomach returning.

"There's an admissions representative from Emerson College in the office, and he wants to see you about your application."

"Emerson?" Aaron muttered to himself. "But I didn't . . ."

The woman turned and started back from whence she came. "He mentioned something about a full scholarship, so I'd get my butt down there if I were you."

Vilma touched his arm. "You'd better get going," she said, looking genuinely excited for him.

He was torn. He really wanted to go to lunch with Vilma, but the potential for a scholarship was something he couldn't pass up. "What about you?" he asked. "I really want to—"

"We can do lunch tomorrow," she said, cutting him off. "Don't worry about me." She turned toward her friends who were still gawking from across the hall. "I'll just grab some lunch with them. No problem, really." Vilma pointed him down the hall. "Maybe you could meet me later—let me know how the interview went?"

"Sure," he responded, stunned by her interest. "I'll meet you at your locker after last period." He was going to turn and wave goodbye, then decided against it. It wouldn't be cool.

But as he turned the corner he lost control, looked back, and waved. Vilma was still watching him and waved back. Her two nosey friends were with her now and they both began to laugh.

As he headed toward the guidance office, he mentally reviewed the college applications he had already sent out. And try as he might, he couldn't remember ever sending one to Emerson.

Mrs. Vistorino was on the phone behind her desk as Aaron entered the office.

"He's in Mr. Cunningham's office," she whispered as she put her hand over the receiver. "Mr. C's gone for the rest of the day."

She removed her hand from the phone to resume her call. "Good luck," she mouthed as he tapped on the office door. Then he turned the knob and entered.

The man's back was to Aaron as he stared

out the window on to the school's parking lot. Aaron gently closed the door and cleared his throat. The man turned and fixed him with a stare so intense it was as if he were trying to see through Aaron's skull to the inside of his brain.

"Uh . . . hi," Aaron said, moving away from the door. "I'm Aaron Corbet—Mrs. Vistorino said you wanted to speak with me?"

He held his hand out to the man. It was something his foster dad had stressed. When you meet someone for the first time, always introduce yourself and shake the person's hand. It shows character, he'd say. The man looked at Aaron's outstretched hand, as if deciding whether it was clean enough to touch.

"And you're . . . ?" Aaron asked, to break the uncomfortable silence.

"Call me Messenger," the man said in a powerful voice, and took Aaron's hand in his.

"It's very nice to meet you Mr. . . . Messenger."

Aaron was suddenly overcome with panic. He couldn't remember ever feeling this way before. He wanted to run—to get as far away from this man as he possibly could. *What's wrong with me now?* he wondered, using every ounce of willpower he had to not yank his hand away.

Messenger released him, and Aaron quickly brought his hand to his side. It felt odd, tingling, like it had when he'd brought Gabriel back from the brink of death. He rubbed his palm against his pant leg.

"I'm glad that I have reached you first," Messenger said, studying Aaron with a strange look in his eyes. "You've matured much faster than most, a sign that you are certainly more than you seem."

Aaron was startled by the admissions rep's words, unsure of their meaning and how he should react. "Excuse me?" he began. "I really don't understand what . . ."

"I believe that you do," Messenger's voice boomed, and for a split second, Aaron saw the man for what he was. He was clothed in armor that seemed to be made from sunlight, and in his hand he held a sword of fire. From his back, enormous wings emanated.

"I am Camael," he said in a voice like the rumbling growl of a jungle cat. "And I have come to protect you."

Aaron closed his eyes and then opened them. Camael had returned to his human state. No armor, no wings, no flaming sword; just a distinguished-looking gentleman with spiky, silver-gray hair and a goatee to match.

"Messenger my ass," Aaron grumbled with disgust. "I should have known. Zeke said you'd be coming for me."

Camael looked perplexed. "Zeke?" he asked.

"Ezekiel," Aaron answered. "Zeke—he's a Grigori . . ."

"A Grigori," Camael said, interested, stroking his goatee. "Then you've already made contact with our kind."

"Right, and he told me the Powers would be after me because of what I am—but I won't go easily."

Camael chuckled. "Spirited, that's good. We'll need a bit of fire if we're going to weather what is to come."

Aaron started to back toward the door, at the moment, confused. "Aren't you one of them—the Powers?"

Camael shook his head as he casually sat on the corner of Mr. Cunningham's desk. "Once it was my holy mission to eradicate the likes of you." He pointed at Aaron and then crossed his arms. "But that was long ago. I've come to save, not destroy. If my suspicions are correct, you have a very important destiny to fulfill, Aaron Corbet."

Aaron suddenly remembered his dream from the weekend—the old man and his tablets. "Does this have anything to do with me building some kind of bridge?"

Camael nodded. "Something to that effect."

Aaron could feel it again, that dangerous curiosity that got him into this predicament. If he'd ignored it originally, he would never have gone in search of Zeke and things would have stayed status quo, or so he tried to convince himself. Well, this time he would put an end to it here and now. He didn't want to hear anything more from Camael.

"Sorry to disappoint you, but it isn't going to happen," Aaron said rather brusquely as he turned to the door. "I don't care what or who you think I am, I'm not having anything to do with this prophecy business." He grabbed the doorknob.

"You might not have a choice," Camael said coolly.

Aaron spun to face the angel. "That's where you're wrong," he barked, attempting to keep his voice down so that none of the insanity being tossed around the office would spill out into the real world. "I've been told my entire freakin' life that *I'm* in control of my future—*me,* Aaron Corbet." He jabbed his thumb at his chest for effect.

"And I've got it all planned out. I'm gonna finish high school, go to a good college, graduate in the top of my class, and get an amazing job that I love." Aaron had no idea what that job would be, but he was on a roll and couldn't stop himself if he tried. "I'll meet a nice girl, get married, and have a bunch a' kids."

Camael said nothing, staring without emotion, allowing him to rant.

"That's how it's going to be, and note—there was no mention of angels, Nephilim, or ancient prophecies. Sorry, there just isn't enough room."

The angelic being stood and moved toward

him. "You're different, Aaron. I can feel it coming off you in waves. Let me help. . . ."

"No," Aaron spat. "I'm through." He pulled open the door. "Go back to Heaven and leave me the hell alone!"

And as he stormed out into the main office, he thought he heard the angel whisper, "That is what we're trying to do."

Camael did not wish to be seen, and so, he wasn't.

He stood on a grassy area in front of the high school beneath the flagpole and watched as students poured out into the world, finished for the day. The young ones had always fascinated him. So full of life, so sure that they had a complete understanding of everything around them and the universe beyond.

To be so certain of anything, he thought, *it must be bliss.*

He remembered how it had been when he first abandoned the host under his command. Even though he knew what he was doing was right, there was still that nagging uncertainty festering in the dark corners of his mind that could not be dispelled. Yes, deep down he felt what the seer foretold was truth, but if he had known in advance the suffering he would have had to endure these many centuries following the prophecy, would he still have taken up the cause?

How many had he saved? How many had he enlightened with the knowledge of their true nature? How many plucked from the destructive path of the Powers? And where were they now? he wondered. Hiding? Waiting for the time when they would be recognized by the eyes of God? And by that account, how many would never see that day of acceptance? How many were slain before even becoming aware they'd been touched by Heaven?

Was it worth it? he reflected, watching the last of the students trickle from their place of learning, milling about in front of the orange brick building in small chattering packs.

And then the one named Aaron Corbet stepped from the school and he experienced an elation the likes of which he had not felt since the day he first bore witness to the seer's words of redemption. *Is this truly the One?* he pondered. Was this the one who would make all the loneliness and pain he had endured worthwhile? If the answer was yes, all he need do was protect him—all he need do was keep him alive to fulfill his destiny and it would all be worthwhile.

But am I strong enough? Camael wondered.

The boy was with a female, very attractive by what Camael had come to understand of human standards: dark hair, skin the color of copper, a radiant smile. And by the looks of it, Aaron was smitten.

This will not do, thought the angelic protector.

There are far more important things for this boy than matters of the heart. He has no idea how much is at stake. Yet, there was something about the girl, the way she moved, the power in her smile—

"Is that the one that has caused so much excitement?" a voice said from behind.

Camael turned to face Verchiel standing just beyond him. He tensed, a weapon of Heaven just beyond his thoughts.

"Of course it is," Verchiel continued. He leaned his head back slightly and sniffed the air catching the scent of the Nephilim that he had followed here. "Doesn't smell much different than any of the others: heavenly power awash in a stink of offal."

Camael chanced a quick glance to see where Aaron and the girl were. They were talking at the end of the school's main walk.

He looked back to see that Verchiel had moved closer.

"Look at him," Verchiel said, "completely oblivious to the world around him. He doesn't even see us. How powerful can he be?"

"It's not that he can't," Camael explained. "He just doesn't want to."

Verchiel mulled this over for a moment, his hawklike gaze still upon Aaron. "I see . . . he denies his true nature. He clings to his humanity while suppressing the angelic."

The girl laughed at something Aaron said, and Verchiel flinched. "I hate the sounds they make," he said, eyes narrowing with distaste. "Don't you?"

"I have spoken with the boy and he rejects it all," Camael said calmly, with just a touch of disappointment for Verchiel's sake. "He wants nothing to do with his heritage."

Aaron and the girl began to move across the parking lot.

"So he is of no immediate threat to us?" Verchiel asked, his head slowly moving as he followed the pair with his unblinking stare.

"He is content with being human," Camael said, watching Verchiel closely.

"His contentment matters not, not in the least," Verchiel said as he turned his attention to Camael. "He still needs to be put down, for his own sake." The angel smiled, fully aware of the effect of his words. "He's far too dangerous to live."

Camael heard the sounds of car doors slamming shut and suspected the couple had gotten into Aaron's vehicle. A burning blade manifested in his hand and he stood his ground, ready to fight if he had to. "Then you will need to go through me," Camael said, an electrical energy radiating from his body and charging the air around them.

"You draw a weapon against me?" Verchiel asked as similar energy began to leak from his eyes and leap from the top of his head.

From the parking lot, car alarms inexplicably

wailed, headlights blazed, and horns blared as if pronouncing the coming of a king. The humans ran about frantically, bewildered, not able to see the battle brewing in their midst.

"We were brothers once, Camael, sharing the same duty to our Heavenly Sire with equal zeal—and this is what it has come to?"

Over the din from the parking lot, Camael located the sound of a single vehicle starting up and driving away. Relieved that Aaron had managed to escape for now, he said nothing.

"I came here to warn you, Camael," Verchiel said, his energy receding. "As former brothers, I believe I owe you at least that."

Camael did not put his weapon away, scanning the area for more of Verchiel's soldiers.

"It's all coming to a resounding close," Verchiel said as he casually slid his hands inside the pockets of his coat and turned away. "After so long, it is finally going to end. A day of reckoning, so to speak."

Camael watched Verchiel begin to walk away. He wanted to call out to him, to make him explain further, but doubted that Verchiel would share any more.

"This moment of truce is over," Verchiel said. "If you should stand in my way, I will not think twice about striking you down," he warned. "Be careful which side you choose, for if you choose wrong—you will share their fate."

The weapon in Camael's hand gradually

returned from whence it came. And as he watched his former comrade recede to nothing, he felt a familiar stirring from within. He knew the feeling well. It was something he had attempted to lock away when deciding to follow the words of the ancient prophecy, something he had held at bay, denying it freedom. But Verchiel's words had drawn it from the shadows and fed its growth.

And its name was doubt.

chapter nine

Aaron drove his '95 Toyota Corolla down Western Avenue and into McDonough Square. He had been in this area of Lynn thousands of times since learning to drive, but had never paid quite as much attention as he did now.

This was Vilma's neighborhood. Febonio's Smoke Shop, Snell's Grocery, Mitchell's Men's Shop—all establishments that he never knew existed until now, all landmarks he would use if he ever had the chance to return.

"It's up here, Aaron. On the left," Vilma said, pointing through the windshield.

Aaron followed her direction and noticed the narrow street just beyond a small store advertising "Everything Brazilian."

"Here?" he asked, snapping on his blinker and slowing down.

"Yep," she answered. "It's a dead end, a real pain to get in and out of."

Aaron waited for the oncoming traffic to slow. A guy in a black van with a crude airbrushed painting of the starship *Enterprise* on its side finally waved him by, and he drove down the dead-end court called Belvidere Place.

"It's the brown house on the end," she said, hefting her bookbag from the floor onto her lap.

The street was very small, only a little wider than his car from nose to backend. A chain link fence across the end of the street separated it from a church and its parking lot beyond. There were eight houses, four on either side, all looking pretty much the same.

Aaron pulled over in front of the last house on the right, put the car in park, and turned to look at Vilma. She was staring straight ahead, her hand starting to move toward the door handle. *She can't wait to get away from me,* he thought. He knew he'd been distracted since leaving school. No matter how hard he tried, he couldn't shake the effects of his meeting with Camael, and he was afraid that his moodiness was a turnoff for Vilma.

"I'm sorry your meeting with the Emerson guy didn't work out," she said, her voice filled with sympathy.

He had told her that the admissions rep had been a jerk and that he had given the man some attitude, probably eliminating himself from the running for a scholarship.

"That's all right," he said with a shrug. "I didn't really want to go there anyway."

He hated to lie to her—it didn't bode well for their future—but what choice did he have? There was no way he could share with Vilma the freak show his life had become over the last week. He had even begun to wonder if it was a good idea to start any kind of relationship with her. The last thing he wanted was for to her to be sucked up into the maelstrom of insanity swirling about him.

The silence in the car was nearly unbearable. Vilma finally opened the door a crack and looked at him. He smiled.

"Thanks for the ride. I really appreciate it," she said, returning his smile. Only, Aaron thought it put his to shame. "I think I had to bring every book in my locker home tonight. My bag's popping at the seams," she said, patting the stuffed nylon bag resting on her lap.

"No problem," he said as he slid the palms of his hands over the smoothness of the steering wheel. "Anytime."

The car door was open but she wasn't leaving. He wondered if there was some gentlemanly thing he was supposed to do like go around to the other side and help her out.

"You know you can call me if you want," she blurted out, as she played with the zipper on her bookbag. "If you wanted to, you know, talk about stuff? Like the Emerson thing—or our paper—I could help you with yours."

Aaron looked at her—really looked at her. Suddenly any nervousness he had been feeling—any lack of self-confidence—was not an issue. In that instant, he decided that not only was Vilma the most beautiful young woman he had ever seen, but also the most real. There were no games with her. She said exactly what was on her mind and he liked that. A lot.

"Now why would you want me to do that?" he asked, looking back to the steering wheel. "I'm sure you have a lot more interesting things to do with your time than talking to me."

She seemed to think about it for a moment and then began to nod her head slowly. "You're probably right. Cleaning up after my cousins, doing laundry, my homework—yeah, you *are* right—I'd much rather do those things than talk with a cute guy on the phone."

He was a bit taken aback, and reached up to nervously scratch the back of his head. "Are you saying that you think I'm cute, or is there some other guy you're going to call?"

Vilma laughed and rolled her beautiful almond-colored eyes. "I thought you were supposed to be the dark, brooding guy—not the big doofus." She shook her head in mock disbelief.

Vilma was laughing at him, but Aaron didn't care. The sound was one of the coolest things he had ever heard, and he began to laugh as well.

"I've never been called a doofus before," he said. He again looked at her. "Thanks."

She reached out to squeeze his arm. "I like you, Aaron," she said.

He had never wanted to kiss a girl so badly. Yeah, there had been that time with Jennine Surrette in junior high, but that was because he had never done it before. Kissing Vilma now would seem almost like his first time—like all the other kisses since Jennine were just practice leading up to this one.

He started to lean his head toward her, his lips being pulled to hers by some irresistible force that he couldn't negate—that he didn't want to negate. Aaron was relieved to see that she seemed to be having the same difficulty, leaning toward him as well.

There came a sudden knock at the passenger-side window, and the spell that was drawing them inexorably closer was abruptly broken.

A little girl, looking like how he imagined Vilma must have looked when she was around seven or eight, peered into the car, smiling. There was an open gap in her comical grin where her front baby teeth used to be.

Vilma shook her fist at the child and she ran off laughing.

"My cousin," she said, looking a bit embarrassed.

The moment was gone, lightning in a bottle—

now free to be captured again some other time. But that was all right. Kissing Vilma could wait—but hopefully, not for too long.

"I like you too," he said, and briefly touched her hand. It felt remarkably warm.

Vilma unzipped the side pocket of her book-bag. She took out a tiny pink pencil and small pad of paper and began to write.

"Here's my phone number and e-mail address," she said as she tore the paper from the notepad and handed it to him. "Call between six and nine, my aunt and uncle kind of freak when anybody calls too late. You can e-mail me anytime and I'll get back to you soon as I can."

He looked down at the phone number. It was as if he had been given the winning number of a billion-dollar lottery—only better.

"You can give me yours later," she said as she got out of the car, lugging her bag behind her. "I gotta get inside and kill my cousin." She turned and leaned back in. "Maybe you can give it to me when we talk tonight," she suggested with another winning smile.

He was about to tell her that it was a deal when he remembered he had to work. "I can't call tonight—gotta work and probably won't get in until after nine."

"Ahh, blowing me off already," Vilma said in mock disappointment.

"Give me that pencil," he ordered.

She handed it to him, smiling all the time,

and watched as he began to write at the bottom of the piece of paper she had given him.

"I'll give it to you now," he said as he finished. He folded the paper and tore away his number. "This way there'll be no mistaking my intentions," he said as he handed her the slip of paper.

"And what exactly are your intentions, Mr. Corbet?" she asked as she slipped the paper into her back pocket.

"In time, Ms. Santiago," he said with a devilish grin. "All in due time."

"Thanks for the ride," he heard her say as she laughed and slammed the door closed.

He watched her walk up to the front porch. She opened the white screen door and turned to wave before she vanished inside.

The clock on the dashboard said that it was close to three o'clock. He had less then five minutes to get across town to work, but it didn't really bother him. As he struggled to back out of the tiny, dead-end street, he realized he wasn't really worried about much of anything right then. Everything was going to work out just fine.

He didn't remember ever before feeling this way.

But it was something he could get used to.

Ezekiel drank from a bottle of cheap whiskey and pondered the question of redemption.

He shifted upon his bed to get comfortable and leaned his head back against the cool plaster wall. He took a long, thoughtful pull off his cigarette.

Redemption. Strangely enough, it was something he thought of quite a bit these days, since meeting the boy.

Zeke reached down to the floor again for the bottle of spirits and brought it to his mouth. Cigarette smoke streamed from his nostrils as the whiskey poured down his throat. It burned, but still he drank.

It was a kind of punishment, he thought as he brought the bottle away from his thirsty mouth and replaced it with the cigarette, a punishment for all that he had wrought.

It's odd thinking about this after so long, he thought, staring at the wall across from him. A cockroach had started to climb the vertical expanse and he silently wished it luck. He could have told the insect directly but the communication skills of a bug were so primitive.

Forgiveness—is it even possible? After the Grigori were exiled, they had tried to make the best of it. Earth became their home. They knew they would never see Heaven again. The idea that they might be forgiven had never even entered his mind—until the day he first saw the boy at the common.

He took another drag from his cigarette and held the smoke in his lungs. There he was, minding his own business, looking through the trash for redeemable cans, when he sensed him—clear across the common he could feel the kid's presence. He'd encountered others over the centuries, but none ever had that kind of effect on him. Aaron was special. He was different.

Zeke released the smoke from his lungs in a billowy cloud. The cigarette was finished and he threw the filter to the floor. He wanted another and considered asking a neighbor to spot him one until he remembered that he already owed cigarettes to several people in the building. He would need to drown the urge to smoke.

What would I say to Him—to the Creator? he wondered as he picked up the bottle. "I'm sorry for messing things up," he muttered, and had some whiskey.

He let the bottle rest against his stomach and gazed up at the ceiling, concentrating on a water stain that reminded him of Italy.

Was saying he was sorry even enough?

Zeke dug through the thick haze of memory to find what it was like to be in His presence. He closed his eyes and felt the warmth of his recollection flood over him. If only there was a way to feel that again—to stand before the Father of all things and beg His forgiveness.

He opened his eyes and brought his fingers to his face. His cheeks were wet with tears.

"Pathetic," he grumbled, disgusted with his show of emotion. "Tears aren't going to do me a bit of good," he said aloud as he brought his bottle up to drink. He leaned his head back and swallowed with powerful gulps. He belched loudly, a low rippling sound that seemed to shake the rafters. "Should'a thought how sorry I'd be before I started handing out makeup tips," he said sarcastically.

The smell suddenly hit him. Smoke. And not the kind he desperately craved. Something was burning.

He rose from his bed and walked barefoot across the room to the door. If Fat Mary down the hall was using her hotplate again, they'd all be in trouble. The woman could burn water, he mused as he opened the door to the hallway.

A blast of scalding air hit him square and he stumbled back, arms up to protect his face. The hall was on fire and quickly filling with smoke.

Panic gripped him, not for his own safety, for he was almost sure the flames could not kill him, but for the safety of the other poor souls who called the Osmond their home.

He stumbled out into the hallway, his hand over his mouth, a bit of protection from the noxious clouds swirling in the air. There was a fire alarm at the end of the hallway, he remembered. If he could get to it, he might have a chance to save some lives.

Zeke pressed himself to the wall, feeling his way along its length.

He could hear the cries of those trapped

inside their rooms by the intense heat.

The smoke was growing thicker. He got down on all fours and began to crawl. The wood floor was becoming hot to the touch, blistering the skin on his hands and knees as he moved steadily forward. He couldn't be far now.

Zeke looked up, his seared and tearing eyes trying to discern the shape of the alarm on the wall—and that was when he saw them. There were two of them, slowly making their way through the smoke and fire.

He tried to yell, but all he could manage was a series of lung-busting coughs.

The smoke seemed to part and they emerged to stand over him, flaming swords at the ready, wings slowly fanning the flames higher.

"Hello, Grigori," said the angel whom Zeke fearfully recognized as one who had helped to sever his wings so long ago.

"We've come to tie up loose ends," said the other.

They both smiled predatorily at him.

And Zeke came to the horrible realization that the fire was the least of his worries.

Aaron pulled his car into the driveway of his home on Baker Street a little after nine o'clock. He switched off the ignition and wondered if he had the strength to pull himself from the car and into the house.

To say that he was exhausted was an understatement. It was the first time he had been back to the veterinary hospital since his language skills had—how had Zeke put it?—blossomed.

It had been insane from the minute he rushed through the door, barely on time. The docs had been running late, and the waiting area was filled with a wide variety of dogs and cats, each with its own problem. There had even been a parrot with a broken wing and a box turtle with some kind of shell fungus.

He had immediately set to work, making sure that everybody had done the proper paperwork and apologizing for the delays.

And it was as if the animals could sense his ability to communicate with them. As he attempted to carry on conversations with their owners, the pets tried everything in their power to get his attention. A beagle puppy named Lily rambled on and on about her favorite ball. Bear, a black Labrador-shepherd mix, sadly told him that he couldn't run very fast anymore because his hips hurt. A white Angora cat called Duchess yowled pathetically from her transport cage that she felt perfectly fine and didn't need to see a doctor. A likely story, Aaron mused, and one probably shared by the majority of waiting animals.

It was constant: Someone or something was yammering at him from the moment he had walked into the place. Aaron wasn't sure if it was scientifically possible, but he was convinced that his head was going to explode. All he could think of was his skull as a balloon filled with too much air. Bang! No more balloon.

Aaron forced himself from the car with a tired grunt. He would have been perfectly happy to have spent the remainder of the night in the car—but he was hungry. He got his backpack from the trunk and began the pained journey to the house.

He smiled as he recalled how he had prevented his brain from detonating at work. The animals had been carrying on, Michelle had him running back and forth to the kennels for pickups and drop-offs, the docs wanted their exam rooms cleaned so they could bring in the next patient. And there he was, on the verge of blowing up, when he thought of her. He thought about Vilma and a kind of calm passed over him. The chattering of the patients became nothing more than droning background noise, and he was able to finish out the evening with a minimum of stress. Just thinking of her smiling face, coupled with what she had said in the car—it was enough to calm him and release the internal pressure.

Maybe I'll e-mail her after I eat, he thought with a grin.

There was a menacing rumble above him and he looked up. Thick gray clouds like liquid metal undulated across the night sky, on the verge of completely blotting out any trace of the moon and stars.

Looks like we're in for a pretty big storm, he thought as he turned his attention to finding the back-door key.

The scream from inside was bloodcurdling.

Aaron hurriedly opened the door and shouldered his way into the house.

"Mom?" he called out. He dropped his bookbag on the floor.

There was another scream, high pitched and filled with terror. It was Stevie, Aaron was sure of it. He tore down the hallway in search of his foster parents and brother.

"Mom!" he called again as he raced through the kitchen. "Dad!"

More screams.

He found his family in the living room, huddled on the floor in front of the television, which showed only static. Lori tightly gripped the thrashing Stevie in her arms, rocking him back and forth, cooing to the child that everything was going to be fine. Gabriel paced beside them, his tail rigid, hackles up.

"What's wrong with him?" Aaron asked. He had never seen Stevie this agitated.

"Theycom!" the child screamed over and over again. "Theycom! Theycom! Theycom!" His eyes rolled to the back of his head, foamy saliva bubbled from the corners of his mouth.

"He's been like this for half an hour," Tom said, panic in his voice. He stroked his son's sweat-dampened hair. "We don't know what he's trying to say!"

"Theycom! Theycom! Theycom!" Stevie bellowed as he struggled to be free of his mother's arms.

"I . . . I think we should call nine-one-one," Lori stammered. There were tears in her eyes when she looked at Aaron and her husband for support.

Tom rubbed a tremulous hand across his face. "I don't know . . . I just don't know. Maybe if we wait a little longer . . ."

Aaron turned from his parents to find Gabriel no longer pacing, but standing perfectly still. The dog looked up at the ceiling and sniffed the air. He began to growl.

"Gabriel? What's wrong, boy? What do you smell?"

A crack of thunder shook the home from roof to foundation. The lights flickered briefly, and then the power quit altogether, plunging the room into darkness.

"Theycom! Theycom!" the child continued to scream inconsolably at the top of his lungs.

"Something bad," Gabriel said with a menacing edge to his bark. *"That's what Stevie is trying to say. Something bad is coming."*

chapter ten

There was another rumble of thunder and the windows in the living room rattled ominously. Aaron began to experience the same overpowering sense of panic he had felt in the guidance office when coming face-to-face with Camael.

"We need to get out of here," he said, gazing up at the ceiling. "We . . . we should get Stevie to the hospital right away."

Gabriel's words echoed through Aaron's head. *"Something bad is coming."*

"I don't know, Aaron," Lori said. "He seems to be calming down." She looked at her child; there was uncertainty and fear in her eyes.

Stevie's struggles were indeed waning. He had screamed himself hoarse but still tried to squeak out his warning.

Tom leaned down and kissed the boy's head.

"I've never seen him like this before, maybe Aaron's right. Maybe we should take him—just in case."

"Good, we'll take my car," Aaron said quickly as he and Gabriel moved into the darkened kitchen.

"He doesn't have any socks on," he heard his mother say behind him. "Let me go upstairs and get his sneakers and socks. I should probably bring his coat, too, just in case . . ."

"We don't have time for that, Mom," Aaron barked. His panic was intensifying. "We have to get out of here right now."

Every fiber of his being screamed for him to get away, to leave everything and run as fast as he could into the night. It took every ounce of his self-control not to leave his parents and little brother behind. Nothing would make him do that, in spite of what his senses were telling him. After so many tumultuous years in the foster care system, the Stanleys were the only people, the only *family,* who'd stuck it out with him, showering him with love, and more importantly, acceptance. . . .

His foster dad came up from behind. "Take it easy, pal. He'll be okay. There's no reason to get crazy with your mother. I'll get his shoes and we'll be out of here in no time."

"No time," Gabriel said suddenly, staring at the kitchen door.

Clack!

They all jumped at the sudden sound as the deadbolt on the kitchen door slid sideways as if moved by some invisible force.

"What the hell is that?" Tom asked, trying to get around his son.

"Go," Aaron said forcefully. "Take Mom and Stevie and go out the front door."

The door began to slowly open with the high-pitched whine that Tom had been threatening to put oil to since the summer, and three men entered on a powerful gust of wind. Aaron's senses were blaring and he winced in pain from their razor-sharp intensity. He knew what these men were. Not men at all.

Angels.

He was enthralled by the way they moved. They didn't so much walk into the house as glide, as though on wheels or a conveyor belt.

"What is *this*?" Tom Stanley hollered, pushing Aaron out of the way. "Get the hell out of my house before I beat the livin'—"

It happened quickly. Tom advanced, fists clenched, intent on defending his home and family. Fire suddenly leaped from an invader's hands and his father stumbled back, covering his eyes as he fell to the linoleum floor.

Aaron couldn't believe what he was seeing. It was just like his dream. The three invaders were holding swords. Swords made of fire.

"Call the police!" his father shouted as he struggled to stand.

Aaron ran to help him. "Get up! You have to get Mom and Stevie out of here."

One of the invaders stalked slowly toward them, his face eerily illuminated by the light of his weapon. There was something unnerving about the way he looked—the way *they* looked. They were deathly pale, almost luminescent in their whiteness, and their features were perfectly symmetrical—too perfect. Aaron felt as though he were looking at mannequins come to life.

"Do we frighten you, monkey?" the invader asked in a voice like nails running down a blackboard. "Does our presence make you tremble?"

"Get away from them!" Lori screamed from the doorway to the living room.

In her arms she held the limp and nearly catatonic Stevie, his eyes large and glassy, like saucers. Gabriel stood by them, tensed, preventing her from entering the kitchen.

Aaron got his father to his feet and pushed him back toward the living room. The stranger raised his flaming sword above his head. Wings dappled with spots of brown dramatically unfolded from his back. Aaron and his father froze, awestruck by the sight of something they once believed to be purely of fiction—of myth.

The angel prepared to strike them down. "We are the Powers—the harbingers of your doom. Look upon us in awe!"

The blade of fire began its descent, and Aaron stepped in front of his father to take the hit.

Suddenly there was a flurry of movement and a yellow-white blur passed over him with an unearthly grace, landing in front of the sword-wielding attacker and snarling ferociously.

Gabriel.

"No!" Aaron screamed as he watched his beloved friend lunge at the supernatural invader.

The dog's jaws clamped down upon the wrist of the angel's sword hand with a wet crunch, like the sound of celery being crushed between eager teeth. The sound made Aaron wince with imagined pain.

The sword of fire tumbled from the angel's grasp to dissipate in a flash before it could touch the floor—and the creature began to scream. The sound was like nothing Aaron had ever heard before, part crow caw, part whale song, part the screech of brakes.

"What is happening?" Lori cried aloud, clutching her moaning child to her.

"We've got to get out of here!" Tom shouted as he lunged toward his family and wrapped his arms protectively about them.

Gabriel dangled from the angel's wrist, growling and thrashing, as if trying to sever the hand from the arm. The angel seemed stunned by the savagery of the animal's attack. The other two, who had remained uninvolved in the background, now stepped forward to assess their comrade's situation.

"It hurts, my brothers!" wailed the Powers soldier as he frantically tried to shake Gabriel loose. "The animal is not as it should be—it has been changed!"

The angel flailed his arm wildly and Gabriel finally released his grip, falling to the floor.

"Gabriel, come! Now!" Aaron yelled.

The Lab stayed where he had landed, in a crouch, baring his fangs and snarling at the angels. A thick black blood, like motor oil, streamed from the injured angel's wounds to form glistening puddles on the yellow-check flooring.

"No," said the dog between snarls. *"Get Mom, Dad, and Stevie out. I will keep these beasts here."*

Aaron was torn. "I'm not leaving you!" he yelled.

But he knew that every second counted. Aaron quickly gathered up his family and ushered them toward the hallway. He would try to get them out the front door to his car and then come back for his friend.

They stepped through the kitchen door and stopped short. Another angel was crouched in the hall, going through his bookbag, its eyes glistening wetly in the darkness. "Going nowhere, silly monkeys," it hissed.

A powerful gust of wind pummeled the house from outside and it creaked and moaned with the force of the blow. Aaron tensed, sensing that something bad was to follow. The front door explosively blew in, torn from its hinges, practically crushing the squatting angel against the wall, and driving Aaron and his family back toward the kitchen in a shower of debris.

Aaron shielded his eyes from pieces of flying matter, and when he looked up he saw that another of them now stood in the doorway, an angel with long white hair. The way this one stood—the way he carried himself—Aaron was certain he was in the presence of the leader, the one Zeke had called Verchiel.

The newcomer cocked his head strangely and surveyed all that was before him. Others slunk into the home behind their leader: all deathly pale, all wearing the same kind of clothes.

There must have been a sale somewhere, Aaron thought perversely, almost starting to giggle. The angels followed Verchiel closely as he strode down the hallway as if he belonged there, and Aaron forced his family back into the kitchen, out of his destructive path.

"What has happened here?" he heard Verchiel ask, in a low, melodic voice that was almost pleasing to the ear.

The Powers soldier held out his wounded arm to his master and averted his gaze. "The animal—it has been altered."

Verchiel moved toward them—toward the family, his dark gaze on Gabriel, and they retreated to the living room.

"Stay away from my family," the dog growled menacingly, baring his teeth and putting himself between the Stanleys and the angel leader.

"*He* has done this to you," Verchiel said in disbelief, looking from the dog to Aaron. "It is worse than I imagined," he whispered. "The Nephilim has spread its taint to a lowly beast."

"I'm not lowly," Gabriel snarled, and leaped at his newest adversary.

In a flash, powerful wings appeared from Verchiel's back and swatted the dog violently away.

The animal yelped in pain as he hit the far wall, narrowly missing the windows, and crashed to the floor.

"See the damage you have already wrought, monster? *This* is why we act," Verchiel growled, his wings slowly flapping like the twitching of a pensive cat's tail before it strikes. "*This* is why the unclean must be purged from *my* world—" The angel paused, considering what he had just said before he continued. "For if allowed to fester, the consequences would be inconceivable."

Aaron left his family to go to his dog's side. "Are you all right?" he asked.

Gabriel struggled to his feet and shook his body vigorously, shedding the effects of his injury like water. *"I'm fine, Aaron,"* the dog said, fixing his gaze on Verchiel. *"And I won't let him hurt you."*

Aaron stood and patted his dog's head.

"That's all right, this is over now."

Gabriel gazed up at his master, a quizzical expression on his canine features.

Aaron addressed Verchiel. "No matter what you think . . . I'm no threat to you or your mission."

Verchiel tilted his head to one side as he listened.

From the corner of his eye Aaron could see that more of the angelic soldiers had moved into the room to encircle him and his family. He didn't react. He didn't want to show any signs of aggression.

"Whatever you've heard—or sensed—about me is a lie. I want nothing to do with Nephilims—or the crazy prophecy that comes with it. I already told Camael, I renounce it. Whatever *it* is, it's not going to be part of my life," Aaron said firmly. "Please, leave my family and me alone."

Verchiel smiled and Aaron was reminded that he was in the presence of something all together inhuman.

"Camael believes you are the One," Verchiel said smugly, moving his head from one side to the other.

"He's wrong," Aaron responded emphatically. "I want nothing more than to have a normal life."

"He believes you to be the one whose coming was foretold in an ancient prophecy, that you are going to reunite the fallen angels with God."

Aaron shook his head vigorously, remembering the old man with the cataract-covered eye from his dream. "I don't know anything about that and I don't care to know."

"Criminals," Verchiel spat. "Those who fought alongside the Morningstar against the Father during the Great War and fled to this pathetic ball of mud, those who disobeyed His sacred commands—those are the ones of whom the ancient writings speak. If this prophecy were to come to fruition, they would be forgiven."

Aaron said nothing. He glanced at his parents who were huddled with Stevie, Verchiel's soldiers surrounding them with their flaming weapons. They appeared to be in shock. He wanted to tell them how sorry he was for bringing this down upon them. He hoped there would be time for that later.

Verchiel shook his head. "Imagine the Almighty looking favorably upon the by-product of angel and animal. It is an insult to His glory."

"I swear you have nothing to fear from me," Aaron said. "Please, leave us alone."

Verchiel laughed, or at least Aaron believed it was a laugh. It sounded more like the caw of some great, predatory bird.

"Fear you, Nephilim?" Verchiel said with what seemed to be amusement. "We do not fear you or anything like you." An orange flame sparked in the palm of his hand and began to grow. "The Powers' mission is to erase anything that would displease our Lord of Lords. This has been our purpose since Creation, and we have performed it well these many millennia."

Verchiel now held an enormous sword of fire, and Aaron heard Lori gasp. "It's a nightmare," she said softly, "some kind of bad dream."

If only that were true, he thought sadly.

Verchiel watched the weapon blaze in his grasp, his eyes of solid black glistening. "And when our mission is finally complete, He shall give us this world—and all who live upon it will know that *I* sit by His side and *my* word is law." The Powers' leader admired his weapon. "But there is still much to be done."

Verchiel pointed the blade at Aaron. "You must die, and so must everything that has been tainted by your touch." He motioned toward Gabriel and then across the room at Aaron's parents and Stevie.

"Listen to what I'm saying," Aaron pleaded, stepping forward. Two of Verchiel's soldiers grabbed him, driving him roughly to his knees. *"Please,"* he begged as he struggled against his captors.

Verchiel still pointed his sword toward Tom, Lori, and Stevie who had again begun to flail in his mother's arms, moaning and crying at the angel's attentions.

"Beg all you like, Nephilim. It will do you no good. You shall be destroyed." He paused, suddenly interested in the cries of the child. "All except the young one," the angel said thoughtfully.

"I think I'll keep him."

Verchiel garnered a certain measure of perverse satisfaction as he watched the Nephilim squirm. This was the savior? The one who was supposed to bring about a peace between Heaven and Earth the likes of which had not been seen since Genesis? It was laughable—yet, there was something about him.

"Bring me the child," he ordered with a wave of his hand.

If there was ever to be peace, it would not be until the enemies of the one true God were turned to ash drifting in the wind. This belief, of his own devising, was the only one he could ever come to imagine.

"Leave him alone!" the one called Aaron shouted, struggling mightily against his captors.

The accursed dog moved defiantly toward him, the skin of its snout pulled back in a ferocious snarl. The blood of angels stained its muzzle.

"Shall we see who has the worse bite?" Verchiel asked, and brought his sword to bear on the dog.

"No!" the Nephilim cried. "Come, Gabriel. Please, come to me."

Hesitantly the dog returned to his master's

side, growling and snarling at the angels who held him. "Good boy," Verchiel heard him say. "It's okay, everything is okay."

Verchiel decided that it was time to show the boy how wrong he was. He motioned toward Uriel, still nursing his wound from the Nephilim's tainted animal.

"The child," he ordered Uriel. "Bring it here."

The angel tore the squalling youth from its mother's arms while Sammael and Tufiel restrained the parents. The cacophony of screams and wails put Verchiel's nerves on edge, but he restrained himself. After all, they were only animals.

Uriel brought the writhing child before Verchiel, holding him by the hair for closer examination. "This one," the wounded angel noted, "seems full of spirit."

Yes, Verchiel thought, staring into the child's unfocused gaze. *He shall serve us well.* He brought the burning sword up beneath the child's eyes and moved the blade back and forth. Its eyes followed the fire attentively.

"A hound perhaps," he said aloud. "You have the eyes of a tracker."

It was then that the Nephilim began to carry on, and Uriel stepped back with the child in his arms.

"Calm yourself, Nephilim," Verchiel said in his most soothing tone. "I told you, I wish the little one no harm."

There is a great power growing within this one, Verchiel observed, studying the Nephilim. He could feel it radiating dangerously from the young man's body.

"The parents, on the other hand," he said slowly as he pointed his blade at the husband and wife. "I have little use for them. And since they have been infected by your presence . . ."

Sammael and Tufiel stepped quickly away from the two as the flame from Verchiel's blade roared to life—and hungrily engulfed the pair in its voracious fire.

Aaron's parents screamed for mere seconds—but it seemed to him an eternity. Their blackened skeletons, burned clean of hair, skin, and muscle, collapsed to the ground in a clumsy embrace.

Verchiel looked to him, seemingly savoring his expression of complete despair. "Now," he said, a hint of a smile on his pale, bloodless lips. "Shall we continue?"

Gabriel tossed his head back and began to howl, and Aaron was certain he had never heard anything quite so sad.

His parents were dead—burned alive before his eyes.

He jarringly recalled the day—his birthday, in fact—when he had stood and stared at his sleeping foster mom in this very room, and thought of her now no longer in his life. His heart raced and he could barely catch his breath.

The pungent aroma of overcooked meat hung sickly in the air, and he did all that he could to keep from vomiting.

Verchiel was saying something, but he wasn't listening. The smoke alarm was blaring from the ceiling above him and he barely heard it. The image of the two people he loved most in the world being consumed by fire kept replaying before his mind's eye as their skeletal remains still smoldered before him.

Disturbingly, Aaron wondered if the fire used by the murderous angels was the same as what he cooked with, or what burned on the head of a match. Maybe it was a special fire, given to those with special identification by high-ranking officials at the pearly gates. Aaron smiled, more like a grimace of sharp and sudden pain. *If I'm so special, maybe I can wield this fire as well.*

He caught movement from the corner of his eye and pulled his gaze from what was left of Lori and Tom Stanley.

Stevie was being taken from the house. The angel—what had he been called? he asked himself. *Uriel?* Uriel was taking his little brother out through the broken front door. But to where? Where were they taking his little brother? He didn't have on any socks or shoes. Aaron thought about trying to follow, but was distracted by the latest nightmare unfolding in the middle of the living room.

They had Gabriel.

Four angels pinned the dog in place while Verchiel stood before them. He still held the sword in his hand—the one he had used to kill Aaron's parents, to burn them to bones.

Gabriel was struggling, foaming at the mouth and snapping his jaws trying to take a chunk out of the creatures that held him. Aaron wanted to cheer his dog on, but found that he just didn't have the strength.

He looked back to his parents. Even the bones were almost gone now and he wondered if his bones would burn as fast. Something called to him. He could hear it echoing far off in the distance, but didn't pay it any attention. He was busy, watching the fire finish the gruesome task it had started.

Again he was called, louder, sharper and Aaron realized that the sound wasn't coming from inside the room, but from somewhere inside his head. He turned to see Verchiel raise the sword above Gabriel. It seemed to be happening in slow motion.

How come everything horrible seems to happen in slow motion? he wondered with building dread.

Again Aaron heard the sound of his name, this time far more forceful. It partially shook him from his stupor, and he came to realize how angry he was. How enraged. They'd killed his parents, taken his little brother. He couldn't let

Gabriel die too. But what could he do? It was just too much for him to bear.

Two angels still held him in their grasp. He was on his knees, his arms pinned behind his back. He felt their hands roughly grab his head. They wanted him to watch, to see Verchiel's blade end his best friend's life.

The voice from inside his mind continued to urge him from his complacency, not in words, but in feeling—raw emotion. He knew what it was that called to him. When he had last encountered it, it had resembled the strangest of serpents, and it had held open its arms to him and he had accepted it.

Now it was older, more mature—stronger.

And as much as he hated to admit it, it was part of him.

A surge of strength coursed through his body and Aaron struggled to his feet, throwing off his captors with extraordinary power.

Verchiel stopped his blade's descent and glared. "You only delay the inevitable," he said, advancing toward Aaron. "But if you are so eager, then you may die before the animal."

And they closed in around him. Each of them summoned some weapon of fire, and Aaron braced himself for their attack. He was prepared to go down fighting.

The windows of the living room exploded inward, showering the room with broken glass as two more entered the fray.

The Powers seemed to be as startled as he. Gabriel broke from those who held him and ran, panting nervously, to Aaron's side. The angel called Camael slowly straightened to his full, imposing height before the shattered window, a burning sword of flame in his hand. And beside him, his skin singed a scarlet red and his hand holding what appeared to be an old Louisville Slugger with multiple six-inch nails pounded into it—turning it into a kind of primitive mace—was the Grigori, Zeke.

"Camael here's been telling me some interesting things about you, Aaron," Zeke said with a cagey wink, breaking the palpable silence. He raised the bat as if to swing at a pitch.

"Told ya you were special."

chapter eleven

It was the sound of a thousand fingernails dragged down the length of a blackboard—only earsplittingly louder. The Powers shrieked their shrill cry of battle and surged toward Aaron's would-be rescuers, weapons afire. For the moment, they had forgotten him. On his hands and knees Aaron crawled to the mound that still glowed red, the mound that used to be his parents. Gabriel, silently and sadly, moved with him. Within the pile of ash, Aaron could see Lori and Tom's skulls still burning, their hollow black gazes accusatory.

"I'm so sorry," he whispered, and reached a shaking hand toward the pyre of ash and bone. He quickly pulled it away as his own flesh was singed by the intensity of the heat.

"It's not your fault," Gabriel said consolingly.

He tried to lick away the hurt from his master's hand.

The intensity of the screams turned him from his parents' remains to the battle being waged in the living room. Aaron was amazed by its ferocity.

Zeke buried the nails adorning his baseball bat into the side of an attacker's head. The angel fell to its knees, twitching and bleeding as Zeke yanked the bat free with a grunt and hit him again before he could recover. Then, satisfied with the death he'd wrought, the fallen angel turned his savage attention to another.

Camael's movements were a hypnotizing blur. He moved among the Powers, hacking and slashing, his fiery blade passing through their flesh with pernicious ease. It was like watching the beauty of a complex dance, but with deadly results. Aaron could see that he was battling his way toward Verchiel, who simply stood, weapon in hand, waiting patiently as his soldiers fought and died around him.

The grisly scene of violence stirred the presence within Aaron. He could feel it roiling around inside him, so much stronger than before, like having the serpentine bodies of multiple eels beneath his flesh. It was excited by the battle—the sights, sounds, and smells.

And then he saw—no, felt—Verchiel staring at him from across the living room. The angel's nostrils flared, as if smelling something in the air. He snarled and began to move toward Aaron.

"It wants to come out, Aaron," Gabriel said by his side. He sniffed him up and down. *"It's inside you and wants to get out."*

Aaron couldn't take his eyes from the angel stalking methodically across the room.

Gabriel suddenly licked his face and, startled, Aaron glared at the dog.

"What's inside of you is inside of me," Gabriel explained. *"I can sense your struggle, but you can't keep it locked up."*

Verchiel was almost upon them.

Slowly Aaron got to his feet, eyes locked on the ominous form of the angel moving inexorably closer. *Maybe I should just let him finish me,* Aaron thought. It was an option he should have considered before his parents were turned to ash. Perhaps if he had offered his life, sacrificed himself, the Powers' leader would have spared them.

"Gotta set it free before it's too late," he heard Gabriel say from his side, an edge of panic in his voice.

Verchiel stopped before Aaron. "It all comes to an end when you are dead," he growled. He raised his weapon and as Aaron stared into his lifeless black eyes, he knew that even if he had offered himself up, his family's gruesome fate would not have changed.

He could feel the heat of Verchiel's sword upon his face as it came at him. A Louisville Slugger blocked its descent. The fire of the blade flared wildly as it cut through the wooden bat, shaking Aaron from his paralysis.

"Get the hell outta here, kid," Zeke yelled as he brought the still-smoking half of the bat up and smashed it as hard as he could into Verchiel's snarling face.

Verchiel was stunned by the fallen angel's blow, but only for an instant. A line of shiny black blood dribbled from his aquiline nose to stain his lips and perfect teeth.

Aaron and Gabriel threw themselves at Verchiel, the intensity of their anger fooling them into thinking that they could help their friend. But Verchiel's wings lashed out from his back again, and the sudden torrent of air threw them back.

Verchiel grabbed Zeke by the back of his scrawny neck and hefted him off the ground with inhuman strength. "It wasn't enough that I took your wings and the lives of your filthy children? Now you want me to end your life as well?"

"Don't!" Aaron shrieked.

Zeke struggled, the piece of broken bat falling from his hand as he writhed. "You have to live, Aaron," he croaked, his voice strained with pain.

"So be it," Verchiel snapped as he ran his blade of fire through Zeke's back in a sizzling explosion of boiling blood and steam.

Zeke screamed, his head tossed back in a moan of agony and sorrow.

Aaron lunged at Verchiel and grabbed his

arm in a powerful grip. "You son of a bitch," he screamed. "You killed him! You killed my parents, you vicious son of a . . ."

"Unhand me, filth," Verchiel said, lashing out with a vicious slap that sent Aaron hurtling across the room.

He landed atop the recliner in the corner of the living room, tipping it over and tumbling to the floor. He fought to remain conscious.

Through eyes blurred with tears, Aaron saw Zeke's twitching body slide off of Verchiel's blade and fall to his knees. A cry like the wail of eagles filled the air, and Camael charged across the room swinging his sword with abandon as he cut his way toward Verchiel. The look upon his face was wild—untamed.

Gabriel was suddenly at Aaron's side, pulling at his clothes. *"Get up,"* he said between tugs. *"You have to set it free. If you don't, you're going to die. We're all going to die."*

Aaron got to his feet and stumbled toward Zeke as Camael and Verchiel battled savagely, their blades blazing hotter, whiter as they clashed. He got to his knees beside the old Grigori and took his hand in his.

"You'll be all right," Aaron told him, his eyes locked on the smoldering black hole in the center of the fallen angel's chest. "I'll . . . I'll help you. Hang on and . . ."

Zeke squeezed his hand and Aaron pulled his gaze from the wound to look into his old eyes.

"Don't worry about me, kid," Zeke said in a whisper. "Nothing you can do except . . ."

"Except what?" Aaron asked, moving closer to the angel's mouth. "What can I do? Tell me."

An explosion sounded from overhead and Aaron instinctively threw his body over Zeke's to protect him. As he gazed up through a cloud of plaster dust and falling debris he saw that Camael and Verchiel had taken their fight outside—up through the ceiling, through the roof—to battle in the sky. He could hear their shrill cries echoing through the stormy night.

"You have to make it true, Aaron," Zeke said, pulling the boy's attention back from the yawning hole above them. "For the sake of all who have fallen . . ."

Zeke's grip upon his hand was intense, and Aaron was overcome with an enormous sadness. He could feel it inside him again, the power churning about at the center of his being. But he didn't want to set it free, for he knew to release it would mean that all he was and all he ever dreamed of becoming would be forever changed.

"You gotta make it happen," the old-timer pleaded.

The presence flipped and rolled inside Aaron, fighting against the restraints that he'd imposed upon it. And he knew that, no matter how hard he tried to deny it, he could not avoid his destiny any longer.

Slowly, gradually, he let his guard down, and the power surged forward just as it had the day he saved Gabriel. An energy coursed through him, a supernatural force that seemed to charge every cell of his body with throbbing vigor.

Aaron opened his eyes and looked down upon his friend—and the fallen angel was smiling.

"It's true," the Grigori whispered. "It's all true."

Aaron felt as if he too were on fire, burning from within. The presence radiated from his body in snaking arcs and he was unsure if mere flesh would be able to contain its power—and still it continued to grow.

His skin felt as though it were melting away. He tore at his clothing, ripping away his shirt to gaze at his naked flesh that was most assuredly afire. Strange black marks were bleeding across his exposed skin from deep within him. With a mixture of fascination and horror, he watched them appear all over his body. They looked like tribal markings, tattoos worn by some fearsome, primitive warrior hundreds and thousands of years ago.

"What's . . . what's happening to me?" he fearfully asked.

Gabriel lay down on the floor nearby and stared, eyes filled with awe. *"Let it happen, Aaron,"* he said consolingly. *"Everything is going to be just fine."*

There was sharp, excruciating pain in Aaron's upper back. "Oh God," he said breathlessly as the agony continued to intensify. Red spots of impending unconsciousness bloomed before his eyes.

He reached over his shoulders, clawing wildly at his back. His fingers touched two tender spots on either side of his shoulder blades: two large, bulblike growths that pulsed with every frantic beat of his heart. The pressure within them was growing. *Gotta let it out!* He raked his nails across the fleshy protuberances, and his hands were suddenly wet as the skin of the growths split and tore open with a sound very much like the ripping of fabric.

Aaron screamed long and hard in a mélange of pain and relief as feathered appendages emerged from his back, languidly unfurling to their full and glorious span.

Breathless, he looked over his shoulder in utter amazement.

Wings.

The wings were of solid black, like those of a crow, and glistened wetly. Muscles that he'd never felt before clenched powerfully and relaxed, and the wings began to flap, stirring the air. He glanced down at the strange markings that covered the flesh of his body, and an eerie calm seemed to pass over him then, a sense that he had finally achieved a serenity he had strived for most of his life.

For the first time, Aaron Corbet felt whole—he was complete.

Gabriel sat watching and waiting. He could barely contain his enthusiasm, his tail furiously sweeping the floor. *"Are you all right?"* the dog asked.

"I've never felt better," Aaron replied, and gazed up through the hole in the ceiling. He could see the shapes of the Powers as they darted and weaved like bats through the night sky in aerial combat with Camael.

The sudden urge to join the fray was intoxicating.

He held out his hand. Images of weapons scrolled through his mind until he saw the one that struck his fancy.

Aaron thought of that weapon and that weapon alone. He thought hard and felt the fire spark in the palm of his hand. The weapon was growing, the fire taking the shape of a mighty battle sword. He held the burning blade aloft, imagining the damage it could do to his enemies.

Again he gazed at the sky above and flexed his newly born appendages.

"Be careful, Aaron," Gabriel said, getting to his feet. *"I'll stay with Zeke. He shouldn't be alone."*

"Knock 'em dead, kid," Zeke said, and gave him the thumbs up.

And Aaron leaped into the air, the virginal wings lifting him from the ground with ease.

As if it were something he was born to do.

† † †

The doubt was gone, driven away by the faith of one who had fallen.

No matter how he tried, Camael could not wipe the memory of Ezekiel's face from his mind. In the open sky above Aaron's home, swords of fire locked in combat, he fruitlessly attempted to push the recollection aside and pressed the attack.

Camael bellowed to the storm-filled night sky and came at Verchiel with his blade of heavenly fire. The Powers' leader dove beneath the swipe of the sword and dropped below, allowing two of his elite to take his place in battle. It seemed as though Camael's former captain did not wish to waste his prowess on a traitor to the cause.

The angel Sabriel swung his weapon, a scimitar that hissed as it cut into the arm of Camael's jacket and the soft flesh beneath. He grimaced in pain and closed his wings tight against his body. Then he let himself quickly drop like a stone, to fall away from his two attackers. And as he descended, the air whipping around him, he again remembered the Grigori.

He had sought out this Zeke that Aaron had spoken of, hoping that somehow the fallen angel would help him to convince Aaron to embrace his destiny. He had tracked the boy's rather powerful residual scent to a dilapidated hotel, where he found the building in flames and the old Grigori about to be murdered by two of Verchiel's soldiers.

Not wanting to fall too far from the current battle, Camael spread his wings to slow his descent and arced heavenward with three powerful thrusts. The Powers' eager cries filled the night. The sky was filled with them, each waiting for a chance to exact revenge on the one who had abandoned their sacred mission to side with the fallen.

He had helped the Grigori against the murderous Powers, impressed by the way the fallen angel had handled himself in battle. He could not recall the Grigori being all that adept at combat, but then again, Earth was a harsh and often brutally violent place and even heavenly beings had to adapt to survive. After escaping from the burning building, Ezekiel had wanted to know why Aaron was so important, why Verchiel was willing to sacrifice so much in order to see him destroyed.

And that was when Camael shared with him the prophecy and Zeke's hard, world-weary features took on a new expression altogether.

It was an expression of hope—hope for forgiveness, hope for redemption, hope for them all. And even though he knew that Zeke was most likely dead, he could not wipe the memory of that moment from his mind. He would use the Grigori's faith as a kind of banner, to chase away the doubt that had plagued him of late and spur him to victory against his enemies.

Exhilarated by Ezekiel's hope, Camael spun unexpectedly, catching one of the four soldiers on his tail unawares. He swung his sword with all his God-given might and severed the angel's head with a single swipe. He watched it spiral to the yard below, bursting into flame as it hit the perfectly manicured suburban lawn.

He imagined the humans in their homes blissfully unaware of the bloody warfare transpiring outside their windows in the skies above. The angelic magic used this night to mask the assault upon Aaron's home must have been great indeed, he mused, still occupied with the thrill of battle.

Seeing their comrade slain, the other three fled, flying off in different directions, and Camael searched the skies for his true enemy, Verchiel. If he were to fall, the Powers would be leaderless and the fight would certainly leave the others—at least until they chose another to command them. This would give him time to take Aaron away, to hide him until he could come to terms with the turn his life had taken.

Rediscovering their courage, two of the three assailants descended from the cover of clouds, their bloodthirsty squeals of excitement giving them away. Camael surged up toward them, meeting their attack head-on with a savagery he had not felt since the Great War. They seemed surprised, as if believing his years among the humans had made him weak.

That wasn't the case at all. He wielded his sword as if it were an extension of his body, swinging in a wide arc, cutting through one's wings, and disemboweling the other. There was a part of him that despised this, for these were soldiers he had once commanded, soldiers who would have followed him into the most hopeless of battles if he had asked. But there was another part that realized that was a long time ago, and he was no longer the same being that had led them—and they were no longer his soldiers. There was cruelty in their eyes, a cruelty that came from the wanton taking of life. If he had stayed on as their leader, he too would have worn the cold stare of superiority—just as Verchiel now did.

A sound from below distracted him. He hovered, riding the currents of wind, and listened carefully. It had come from Aaron's house, and the horrible thought that Verchiel might have slain the Nephilim entered his mind.

Again came the sound and he recognized it for what it was. It was a cry of battle—a war cry.

From the hole in the structure's roof something emerged. It moved with incredible speed, on wings as black as a moonless sky. It wielded a weapon of fire and its exposed flesh was covered in markings that Camael recognized as angelic sigils, markings worn only by the greatest of Heaven's warriors.

Camael suddenly understood what he was seeing—who he was seeing. It was the bearer of hope for the future made flesh. Aaron Corbet had completed the transformation. He stared in awe as Aaron soared closer. Never had Camael seen one like this—so full of power—and he couldn't help but wonder who of the heavenly host could have sired one so magnificent.

The angels of the Powers were drawn to this new creature like sharks to blood-filled water. They circled their prey, briefly assessing its weaknesses, then attacked. And Camael watched in wonder as Aaron defended himself.

The Nephilim was awesome to behold, his bony wings spread wide as he darted about the sky, laying waste his attackers with uninhibited zeal.

"That is what you believe will save us all?" came a voice from behind, startling him.

Camael whirled, sword at the ready. This was the second time in a day that he had let Verchiel sneak up on him. The Powers' leader was close. Dangerously so.

"I will see it dead and burning." Verchiel scowled as he thrust a dagger of fire into Camael.

And he could do nothing but accept the blade, feeling the heat of the weapon break the surface of his flesh and begin to cook the meat of him from the inside. The pain was sudden and blinding, and he didn't even have a chance to cry out as he fell from the sky, surrendering to the black embrace of unconsciousness before striking the ground below.

Verchiel watched the traitor fall toward the embrace of Earth.

"It did not have to end this way," he said regretfully. "This world could have been *ours* if your mind had not been so poisoned by the delusions of inferiors."

One of his soldiers cried out pitifully, and Verchiel returned his attention to the aerial battle at hand.

"The Nephilim," he cursed, watching another of his elite soldiers fall to the prowess of the creature's blade.

How is it this monster fights so fiercely? he asked himself, watching with perverse fascination as it moved through the air on wings of black as if by second nature. It was hard for him to imagine that this nightmarish joining of Earth and Heaven believed itself merely human only a few short days ago.

Another of his soldiers cried out in defeat and fell from the sky afire. The Nephilim's style was crude, erratic, lacking in discipline—yet it fought with an unbridled savagery effective against those who knew not what to expect. The Powers had grown soft over the centuries, untested against a true adversary, but Verchiel knew this foe. Here was the personification of all he'd been fighting against, all that he despised, and he yearned to see it finally vanquished.

To destroy this creature, this symbol of a perverted future too horrible for him to imagine, would be the greatest victory of all. Kill the Nephilim and the prophecy would die with it.

Verchiel still held the dagger he had used to kill his former commander. With a thought, he willed the blade away and summoned another weapon, one he considered sacred. It had not been used since his battle against the armies of the Morningstar. He called this broadsword Bringer of Sorrow, and it was for only the most profound and important of battles.

This was to be such a battle.

The sword materialized in his hand and he pointed it up toward the kingdom of Heaven. And with arcane words used by his kind to bend the elements to their will, he called down a storm upon the world of God's man, a storm to aid him in the defeat of the most horrible of evils.

A storm to wash away the malignant blight of prophecy.

chapter twelve

The storm cover above his neighborhood had grown dense with dark steely clouds that appeared substantial enough to touch. Aaron maneuvered through them, water vapor lightly dampening his bare skin, invigorating him for the next wave of attack. The Powers had suddenly retreated, using the concealing clouds to hide and most likely regroup. Aaron imagined them lying in wait to take him by surprise, and he was ready.

He gazed about the expanse of sky over Baker Street, trying to understand the events of the last several minutes. He had wings. He was flying. And he was involved in a fight for his life, hundreds of feet above his home. It was insane—a thing of bad dreams. Yet he knew it was real.

The Powers had been relentless, coming at

him from all sides. And he had fought them well. With his sword of fire he battled as though it were something he had done every day of his life, as if it were something he was meant to do.

Once he had accepted the transformation, the otherworldly presence had filled his mind with incredible knowledge. He remembered things that he had never known. Aaron suddenly knew the Powers, not just as heavenly beings bent on punishment and destruction, but as warriors who once served a noble cause.

Thunder rumbled and the gray skies were eerily illuminated by a flash of lightning. His eyes scanned the rolling clouds. *More Powers tricks?* he wondered as he looked for signs of imminent attack.

The winds were increasing in strength, and he was buffeted by their force as he continued to search the sky for his enemies. A crack of thunder that he felt from the top of his head to his toes shook the air, and lightning lit the sky. It was a full-fledged storm now, powerful winds, lightning, rain, and thunder. And still the Powers were nowhere to be found.

Aaron gazed with curiosity at the ceiling of churning weather above him and soared upward with powerful thrusts of his ebony wings. He broke through the storm cover and looked beyond his neighborhood. He was not at all surprised to see a calm, star-filled night above the city of Lynn—everywhere except over Baker Street.

He gasped in sudden pain as something hidden in the clouds below grabbed his ankle and viciously yanked him downward. He lashed out blindly with his sword and the hold upon him was relinquished, but not before he found himself back within the raging storm.

The wind howled and the rain fell in sheets. *Heaven is crying,* Aaron thought distractedly, not sure where such an idea would have come from. And before he had the chance to think about it further, above the wail of the winds and the hiss of torrential rain, he heard a powerful voice call out to him.

"Nephilim!"

Aaron twirled in the air, searching for the source, but knowing full well who it would be.

Verchiel emerged from the storm, an awesome sight to behold, white wings carrying him through the turbulent air with ease. He held aloft an enormous sword of fire that sizzled and spat as the rain fell upon it.

Aaron looked nervously at his own weapon and wondered if it would be wise to summon something larger.

"Your time is at an end," the Powers' leader bellowed.

The storm raged harder and Aaron found it difficult to stay aloft.

"I will sweep away your existence like so

much dust in the wind," Verchiel said as he turned his pale features toward Heaven and spread his arms wide.

Lightning zigzagged from the sky, a fracture of luminescence that struck the side of Aaron's home while he looked on in horror.

"No!" Aaron screamed as he fought the raging winds to descend. *Gabriel, Zeke*—his mind raced.

It sounded like the crack of an enormous whip as another bolt descended, and the roof exploded in a flash of white and began to burn. So overwhelmed was he that he became careless. New instincts warned him not to turn his back on Verchiel, but he paid them no mind. He had to get to his friends; if there was anything he could do it had to be now.

Aaron was grabbed from behind, his arms and wings pinned against his body. He watched helplessly as his sword tumbled from his grip to evaporate in the air below.

"This is but the beginning," the angel whispered maliciously in his ear.

Verchiel's breath smelled of spice and decay, and it made Aaron want to gag. He strained his every muscle, to no avail. The Powers' leader was remarkably strong. The mighty storm winds buffeted them, blowing their bodies about like corks caught in a river current. And still he struggled.

Aaron screamed in rage, tapping into the

primal emotion that now coursed through him. He thrashed violently and rammed his head back in a brutal blow to the unsuspecting Verchiel's face.

It was just enough to loosen the angel's grip upon him, and Aaron was able to twist his body around. He looked into his attacker's sneering face, into the eyes of solid black—and in their limitless depths he saw the deaths of thousands.

They were just like him, still children, unaware of the heritage that had marked them for death. Aaron could feel their pain, their desperation, their fear of what they were becoming.

And how was their terror addressed? How were these beings of Heaven and Earth helped to understand their true origins? Only with more horror, as Verchiel and his soldiers came for them. And they were killed, cruelly, methodically, all in the name of God.

Thunder boomed and Aaron freed one of his arms and raked his nails down the angel's face, snagging one of those horrible, bottomless black eyes. Verchiel shrieked above the wail of the storm, his cry like that of a mournful seabird. He recoiled and grabbed at his injured face.

Aaron pushed himself away from his attacker, pure adrenaline pumping through his body—and something more. He chanced a glance below and saw that his house was on fire and part of the roof had collapsed. His anger intensified and he began to scream, a frightening sound incapable of being produced by human vocal cords.

Verchiel continued his taunts. "And when you are dead, we shall move through this city like a firestorm and everywhere you've been, everyone you've had even the slightest contact with—all will be washed away in torrents of fire."

Aaron flew at Verchiel, flaming sword forming in his hand, poised to strike. "You killed them," he shrieked, remembering the faces of those the angel had slain throughout the ages—as well as his own loved ones.

Verchiel blocked his blows with blinding speed, an evil grin slowly spreading across his pale features. The four bloody furrows Aaron had dug into the angel's face had already begun to heal.

"Yes, I did, and it is just the beginning," Verchiel said with an emotionless smile as he fought back with equal savagery. "You are a disease, Aaron Corbet." Verchiel spat his name as if it were poison on his tongue. "And I will cut from the body of this world all you have infected."

Aaron dove beneath the angel and went at him from behind. "All this death—," he began.

Verchiel spun with incredible swiftness. Aaron just managed to duck as the angel's blade passed over his head. He could feel its heat on his soaking scalp.

"—you do it in the name of God?" Aaron asked incredulously.

"Everything I do," Verchiel said with a hiss, fury etched into his scarred features, "I do for Him."

"What kind of god do you serve?" Aaron questioned, struggling to avoid the angel's thrusts, hoping Verchiel's anger would make him careless. "What kind of god would allow you to murder innocents in his name?"

Aaron delivered a blow to the angel's face, rocking his head back and to the side. A wicked thrill went through his body as he watched the angel recoil from the force of his strike. Before the transformation, he wouldn't have lasted two seconds against this berserk force from Heaven, but now Aaron believed that he could at least give Verchiel something to remember him by.

Verchiel spat blood from his wounded mouth and lunged forward, swinging his blade. His attack was relentless, driving Aaron back and away. Aaron blocked the pitiless descent of the broadsword, the blows so forceful that they began to fragment his own blade, finally causing it to disintegrate in his hand.

"Surrender, monster," Verchiel said in a voice as smooth as velvet. "It is God's will." The angel prepared to cut him in half.

Aaron flexed his wings and propelled himself toward Verchiel, driving his shoulder into the angel's stomach.

He grabbed Verchiel's wrist, preventing the sword of fire from descending.

"Is it His wishes you're following, Verchiel—or yours?" he asked as they struggled within the grip of the storm.

Verchiel brought a knee up and slammed it into Aaron's side. He felt the air from his lungs explode and his hold upon the angel's wrist falter.

"I am the leader of the Powers," he heard Verchiel say over the intensifying weather. "The first of all the hosts to be created by the Allfather."

Aaron wanted to call up another weapon to defend himself, but the burning pain in his side and lungs barely made it possible for him to stay aloft. He didn't want to die, to become yet another of the poor souls to fall beneath Verchiel's sword.

Verchiel came at him, sword in hand. He raised the great blade above his head. "His wishes—my wishes," he said, eyes wild with bloodlust.

The winds raged, blowing Verchiel back as he prepared to bring the sword down upon Aaron. "They are all one and the same," he said, straining against the exhalation of nature in turmoil that he had turned loose.

Aaron feebly managed the beginnings of a weapon to continue the struggle, when there was an explosion of sound that seemed to encompass all the heavens. It was a sound Aaron imagined might have been heard at the dawn of creation.

A bolt of lightning arced down from the sky, and he shielded his eyes from the intensity of its resplendence. Like the skeletal finger of some elemental deity composed entirely of crackling blue energy, it roughly tapped the top of Verchiel's head, as if to show its displeasure.

The angel screeched in pain as the lightning invaded his body, to explode free from the sole of a foot. His body seemed to glow from within, his mouth agape in a scream drowned out by the ruckus of the storm. Verchiel exploded into flames, his body no longer able to contain the raging power coursing through it. And, like Icarus, who had flown too close to the sun, he fell from the sky.

"One and the same—are you sure about that?" Aaron asked Verchiel, watching the blazing form of the Power as it spiraled earthward. Then he turned his attentions to the heavens above.

"Are you really sure?"

Verchiel lay upon his side on the cold, damp ground, wracked by a pain the likes of which he'd never felt before. His body, charred black by the power of the lightning strike, smoldered as it cooled in the evening air.

He rolled onto his back to gaze up at the

heavens where his Master resided.

The storm clouds were breaking apart, the angelic magic used to manipulate the weather in all its fury dissipating like wisps of smoke carried away by the wind.

"Why?" he croaked, slowly raising his charred arm, reaching a beckoning hand out to the star-filled night.

But the Creator was silent.

And then they were there, the faithful of his host—those who had survived, looking down upon him, their faces void of emotion. They bent to lift him from the ground, laying the burden of his weight upon their shoulders. And they bore him up into the sky away from the battleground, away from the scene of his most heinous defeat.

"Why?" he asked again, carried closer to the place where his Father dwelled, but still so far that He did not answer.

"Why have you forsaken me?"

The ground grew steadily closer, and Aaron flexed the newly developed muscles in his back. His wings flapped once, and then again to slow his descent.

He touched down on a small patch of lawn in front of the house, falling forward in a scramble to reach the smoking wreckage that had once been his home.

"Stevie?" he screamed, running up the walk that was littered with pieces of burning shingles and wood. Maybe they left him. Maybe they decided they didn't want the little boy after all. "Stevie? . . . Gabriel?" he called frantically into the ruins.

"Gabriel," Aaron called again as he cupped his hands to his mouth, desperate for something of his family to have survived. "Gabriel, Zeke—are you there?"

He sensed an angel's presence behind him and spun around, a new weapon sparking to life in his waiting hand. He had already slain many heavenly beings today, and had no problem adding another to the tally.

"Stay away from me," he warned.

Camael limped closer, paying no heed to his threat. "The child is gone," he said.

The angel looked like hell, his face and clothing spattered with drying gore. He was pressing a hand against a wound in his chest, trying to stem the flow of blood.

"Where is he?" Aaron asked as a combination of emotions washed over him. He was truly glad that his foster brother was still alive, but an awful dread filled him when he thought of who had taken him.

Camael stumbled closer. "The Powers . . . took him. I tried to stop them but—" He removed his hand from the wound and carefully examined it. "I was having some difficulty of my own." From his back pocket he produced a white handkerchief and placed it beneath his coat against the injury. "And no, I do not know where they have taken him."

The angel seemed to fall forward. Aaron reached for him but Camael caught himself on the twisted remains of the wrought-iron porch railing.

"Are you okay?" Aaron asked.

Camael nodded slowly, his eyes studying him. "You're certainly a sight to behold," he said with a dreamy smile. "One that I've yearned to witness since . . ."

Aaron held up his hand to quiet the angel. He didn't want to hear anymore, especially now.

Gabriel bounded out from behind the house calling his name excitedly. Aaron's face lit up at the sight of his canine friend and he knelt to embrace the dog.

"You're okay," he said as he stroked the animal's head and kissed the side of his face. "Good boy, good dog."

"I'm glad to see you, too," Gabriel said, *"but you have to come quick."*

Gabriel pulled away and trotted to the corner of the house.

"Gabe?" Aaron said, following.

"He doesn't have much time left," the dog said as he disappeared around the house into the backyard.

Zeke was lying very still in the middle of the yard beside the swing set, Gabriel sitting attentively by his side.

"I got him out of the house after the lightning hit—but I think he's going to die." The dog looked at Aaron, sadness in his rich, caramel eyes. *"Is he going to die, Aaron?"*

Aaron knelt down in the grass beside the fallen angel and gently took his hand. "I don't know, Gabe," he said. Zeke's hand was cold, like a stone pulled from a mountain stream. "I . . . I think he might."

"Oh," the dog said sadly, lying down beside the Grigori. *"I thought maybe you could do something for him."*

Zeke's eyes slowly opened. "Look at you," he said, a hint of a smile on his weathered features. Zeke gave Aaron's hand a weak squeeze. "All grown up and everything." He began to cough violently and dark blood frothed at his lips. "Damn," he said as he reached up to feebly wipe away the blood. "That don't feel so hot."

Aaron was in a panic. "What should I do?" he asked Zeke, squeezing his hand. "Should I call for an ambulance or . . ."

Zeke shook his head and the blood ran down the sides of his mouth. He didn't seem to notice—or maybe he just didn't care. "Naw," he said with a wave of his hand, his voice starting to sound more like a gurgle. "Too late for that."

Camael had joined them, and Aaron looked to him for guidance. "Is there anything . . . anything we . . . I can do to help him?"

The angel shook his head of silvery hair and

closed his eyes. "The Grigori is dying. Verchiel's blade must have struck something vital."

Zeke gasped and began to convulse violently.

Aaron clutched his hand tighter and leaned in closer. "Zeke?" he asked. "Does . . . does it hurt you?"

"It's okay, kid," he said. His voice was weak, practically a whisper. "Pretty much had my fill of this place anyway."

The fallen angel went silent for a moment, his eyes gazing unblinkingly up at the star-filled sky.

"But I do got something to say," he said, turning his gaze from the heavens to Aaron.

"What's that?" he asked.

Zeke swallowed with difficulty and took a long, tremulous breath. It sounded full of fluid. "I want to say I'm sorry . . . ," he said, his voice trailing off in a gurgling wheeze.

Aaron didn't understand. "For what? What are you sorry for?"

The Grigori seemed to be gathering his strength to answer. "For everything," he said, straining to be heard. "I want to tell you that I'm sorry for *everything* I've done."

At first Aaron wasn't at all sure what he was supposed to do—but suddenly, like the lightning that knocked Verchiel from the sky, it became excruciatingly clear.

Aaron knew exactly what needed to be done.

In all his life, he had never been so certain of anything.

His body began to tingle, the hairs on his arms standing at attention as if he were about to receive the world's largest static shock. He held Zeke's hand and felt the energy begin to move, flowing from the swirling force that seemed to have settled in his chest, down his arm and into the fallen angel.

Zeke went suddenly rigid, but still Aaron held him. He watched in amazement as cracks began to appear in the facade of the Grigori's flesh, from which a brilliant white light shone.

Gabriel leaped to his feet and backed away. *"What's happening to his skin?"* he barked. *"What's happening?"*

But Aaron did not answer.

What had once been flesh fell away from Zeke's body like flecks of peeling paint, and what lay beneath pulsed with a radiance amazing to behold.

This is what it's all about, Aaron thought as he squinted through the white light, still holding tight to his friend's hand.

No longer did Aaron gaze upon a fallen angel, banished to Earth, dying of injuries sustained while trying to protect him. Now he beheld a being of awesome beauty, its body composed entirely of light.

This is what he must have looked like before his fall, Aaron thought, almost moved to tears by the glorious sight.

Bootiful, Aaron thought, remembering his little brother's praise.

The angel Ezekiel gazed up through the milky haze of light, his eyes wide with expectation. And Aaron realized what had yet to be said—what needed to be said in order to set his friend free.

"You're forgiven," he whispered in the language of messengers, and felt warm tears of even warmer emotion trail from his eyes to run down his face.

He released his friend's hand and the aura of energy surrounding him grew in intensity, brighter, warmer. Aaron got to his feet, moving away from the spectacle of rebirth unfolding before him.

Ezekiel rose up from the ground on delicate wings of sunlight. And he turned his beatific face up to the heavens and smiled.

"Thank you," said a voice in Aaron's mind like the opening notes of the most beautiful symphony imaginable. He was overwhelmed in its flow of unbridled emotion.

Then, in a flash of white, like the birth of a star, Ezekiel was gone, restored to a place long denied him.

Forgiven.

chapter thirteen

Drained, Aaron fell to his knees upon the lawn. His eyes were closed but still he saw the beautiful image of Ezekiel burned upon his retinas. He started to relax and felt the wings on his back begin to recede, the appendages of cartilage and feathers disappearing beneath the flesh of his shoulder blades. His skin began to prickle and he opened his eyes to see that the black markings on his arms and chest had begun to fade as well.

Gabriel came to him, tail wagging so furiously that it looked as though the dog had no control over his back end. He dug his head beneath Aaron's arm and flipped it with his snout, demanding to be petted. *"That was nice, Aaron,"* the dog said happily. *"You let him go home."*

Aaron looked to Camael. "What the hell just

happened?" he asked, struggling to stand on shaking legs. "What did I do?"

The angel was looking up into the sky with longing on his soiled, yet still-distinguished features. "There is no more doubt, Aaron Corbet," Camael said, shaking his head, looking from the sky to him. "You are the One whose coming was foretold so long ago. Finally you have come to—"

"What did I do?" Aaron demanded to know.

The angel pulled at his silvery goatee as he spoke. "You have the power to grant absolution," Camael explained, a hint of a smile playing on his features. "Any who have fallen from the grace of God will be granted forgiveness in your presence, as long as they have seen the error of their ways."

"That's nice, Aaron," Gabriel said, looking up at his master, tail still happily wagging. *"Isn't it nice?"*

"Yeah, it's nice. So they're forgiven, what does that mean?" Aaron asked the angel. "Where did Zeke go?"

Camael again gazed upward. "He has returned home."

Aaron, too, looked into the sky. There was no longer any sign of the storm that had battered his neighborhood. "You're telling me that Zeke went back to Heaven."

"Your people have many colorful names for where he has gone: Paradise, Elysium, Nirvana, the happy hunting ground—Heaven is but one of them," Camael explained.

Aaron mulled this over. "And I sent him there?"

Camael pointed at Aaron with a long, well-manicured finger. "You are the bridge between the fallen and God."

"God, huh?" Aaron slipped his hands casually into the back pockets of his jeans. He gazed toward what was left of his home, painfully remembering what had been done to it, to his parents—all in the name of God. He scowled and stormed away. "Y'know what?" he said, walking around the house to the front. "I don't think so."

Camael followed. "You can't run away from this, Aaron," he said, catching up to him. "It is your destiny. It was written of—"

Aaron spun around, stopping the angel cold. "Thousands of years ago," he finished. "I know all about it and I'm not too sure how happy I am serving a God who would allow *this* to happen." He gestured to the still-smoldering remains of his home. "Not to mention the hundreds—maybe thousands—of others He's allowed Verchiel to kill in His name." Aaron was furious, ready to take on the Creator Himself if necessary. "You tell me how I'm supposed to do this."

The Stanleys' neighbors had begun to emerge, cautiously making their way from their homes to view the devastation that they believed was caused by a storm.

Aaron gazed at what remained of the only

home he'd ever known, both he and the angel watching as the last of the fire burned down to glowing embers.

"I understand your anger," Camael said.

Climbing the crumbled brick steps to where the front door once stood, Aaron stepped over what was left of the entryway into the rubble of his home. "Do you, Camael? Do you really understand?" He stood where the living room once was—where his parents had died. "Up until a few days ago I didn't believe in Heaven, angels, or flaming swords—never mind God." He kicked at a piece of wood that still glowed red. "And now I find out I'm part of some elaborate plan to reunify Heaven, to reunite all of God's children so they can be one big happy family again."

He remembered the boring simplicity of movie night with his foster family, and almost began to cry. But he was too angry for tears.

"How am I supposed to do this for Him when He couldn't even bother to save my family? Can you tell me that, Camael, because I'm really curious."

The sad wail of sirens could be heard in the distance.

"The Almighty," Camael began, "the Almighty and His actions or lack thereof . . . they are part of a much larger scheme. We may not understand it but—"

"The Lord works in mysterious ways,"

Aaron interrupted sarcastically. "Is that how you're going to try and explain this? That it's all part of some big picture that we're not privy to?"

There were neighbors in the street in front of the demolished home. There was fear in their eyes. Aaron could practically hear the thoughts running through their minds. *How could this have happened without me knowing? I didn't even know it was raining. Was there an explosion? I live right next door. This could have happened to me. I hope everyone is all right.*

"I know how hard this must be to grasp in a moment of tragedy. It is a quandary I, too, have come to ponder in my time upon this world." The angel walked to an area of collapsed wall and squatted before it. "The Father is aware of everything," he said, reaching beneath the plaster. "No matter how harsh or random things may appear, He does have a plan."

Camael pulled something from the rubble and brought it to Aaron. It was a broken frame and undamaged within it was a picture of his entire family. They were all wearing Santa hats, even Gabriel. Aaron took it and gazed at the happy image. He remembered when it was taken two years ago—how appalled he had been to have to wear the stupid hat. He had been even more mortified when the Stanleys had used the picture for their Christmas card that year.

Aaron carefully took the picture from the

frame, a remembrance of a life now horribly altered by an ancient destiny.

"Sometimes the bad must precede the good," Camael said in another attempt to make him comprehend the machinations of the Creator. "Do you understand what I'm trying to say?" he asked.

Gabriel sniffed about the burned remains of what had been the recliner, sticking his nose beneath its twisted metal skeleton in search of something. Aaron was about to tell the dog to be careful when Gabriel pulled a filthy tennis ball from beneath the chair.

"Look, Aaron!" he said excitedly, his speech distorted by the ball rolling around in his maw. *"I've found my ball. I thought I'd lost it forever!"* The dog eagerly let the ball fall from his mouth. For a brief moment his friend was happy, all the sadness of the past few hours pushed aside.

Aaron didn't like Camael's explanation of how things worked, but guessed he had no choice but to accept it. There was method to God's madness, so to speak.

He looked at the picture of his family one more time, then folded it and slid it into his back pocket.

"I have to find my little brother," Aaron said, looking to the angel that stood at his side. "Will you help me get him back?"

The fire engines screamed onto Baker Street,

lights flashing, sirens howling as if mourning all the sadness they'd borne witness to.

"I will do that," Camael said with little emotion. Aaron might as well have asked him if he wanted milk or cream in his coffee.

Gabriel brought the ball to Aaron and let it drop at his feet. He wagged his tail as he leaned his head forward and lovingly licked his hand. *"Don't worry,"* he said. *"We'll find Stevie. You'll see, Aaron, everything will be fine."*

And as he gazed around at the smoldering ruins of his home, reflecting upon the shambles his life had become, thinking about the unknown that was the future ahead, Aaron wasn't so sure that anything would ever be fine again.

epilogue

"Are you sure about this, Aaron?" Principal Costan asked from behind the desk in his office at Kenneth Curtis High.

It had been two days since the supposedly freak lightning storm took the lives of his foster mother, father, and little brother, and Aaron felt it would be best that he leave school, and the city, as soon as possible.

Aaron nodded as he handed the man the papers he had signed officially withdrawing from Ken Curtis. "I'm sure, sir. I just can't stay around here anymore. It's for the best."

It had been the same at the animal hospital, people asking him if he was certain that this was what he really wanted to do. Of course it wasn't, but the threat of the Powers had left him little choice.

Mr. Costan took the papers and frowned.

"Y'know, it's none of my business, but running away from something isn't going to make it any—"

"I'm not running away," Aaron cut in, perturbed at his principal's suggestion.

The disturbing image of Verchiel and his soldiers descending from the sky, fire in their hands, laying waste to the school and everyone inside it, played out in his mind.

"There are just too many memories here," he said. "I think I'd seriously benefit from a change of scenery." And the quicker he got on the road, the quicker he could find Stevie, he thought as he watched the man behind the desk across from him.

Camael had explained why the Powers had taken his little brother. It had something to do with the handicapped—"the imperfect" as Camael had coldly referred to them—having some kind of sensitivity to the angelic, making them perfect servants. The thought of his little brother acting as a slave to the monster Verchiel both chilled him to the bone, and made him seethe with anger. He had to find Stevie before any harm could come to him.

The principal scrutinized the completed documents and placed them in an open folder on his desk. "Very well then. It doesn't appear that I can change your mind. And since you're now of legal age . . ." Mr. Costan closed the folder and stood, extending his hand.

Aaron stood as well and took the principal's offered hand.

"Good luck, Aaron," Costan said, "and if you ever want to come back to finish your senior year, I'm sure we could work something out."

Aaron shook the man's hand briefly and then let it go. "Thanks for everything," he said as he turned and quickly left the office, desperate to escape before the principal tried yet again to make him reconsider his decision.

The clock in the reception area said that it was a little after nine. If he hurried, he could clean out his locker, drop off his books, and be out of the school before first period ended.

The halls were empty as he made his way to his locker for what would be the last time. Memories flooded through his mind. He remembered the first day of freshman year as if it were only a few months ago. The place had seemed so huge then; he thought he'd never learn his way around. Aaron smiled sadly—if only his problems had remained so inconsequential.

At his locker he removed the textbooks and gathered his belongings, double-checking to be sure he hadn't left anything behind. He slammed the metal door closed for the final time, and was overcome with an intense sadness and anger.

It isn't fair, he thought. He was supposed to leave this place just like everybody else: finish up senior year, attend graduation wearing that brightly colored gown and the seriously goofy mortar board, and then go off to college.

But fate had dealt him a cruel hand, and his destiny lay down a different path altogether.

Aaron lashed out and kicked the locker to release some of his pent-up frustration. The sound was thunderous in the empty halls. He lost his grip on the books beneath his arm and they tumbled to the floor in disarray. Aaron felt like screaming, but somehow managed to control himself. He bent down to retrieve his belongings with a heavy sigh, feeling like a complete moron. An angry, complete moron.

"Do you want some help?"

Aaron quickly looked up, feeling the sudden weight of sadness press him even further into depression. This was why he'd wanted to get out before the first period ended. He hadn't wanted to see her.

Vilma Santiago knelt down beside him and helped him gather his books.

"Thanks," he said, trying as hard as he could not to make eye contact.

"You were leaving without saying good-bye, weren't you?" she said softly as she handed him his history book.

He looked at her then and saw that her eyes were moist and red. She had been crying.

"I don't know how, but I knew you were out here." She showed him a piece of pink paper, a hall pass. "I said I had to go to the bathroom."

She smiled and laughed a bit. Though filled with sadness, it still was a disturbingly beautiful sound, and his heart ached. Nervously he straightened the stack of books, unsure of how he should address her accusation.

"I didn't want to go through the whole good-bye thing," he said, wishing with all his heart that he could tell her he was only trying to keep her safe. "I just can't deal with anything else that's sad."

He was dying inside. Of all the things he was leaving behind, Vilma was the thing that pained him the most. There was no one else here to say good-bye to. Aaron stood, holding the stack of books beneath his arm.

"For what it's worth," she said with a sniffle, "in Brazil . . . when my mother died, I didn't think I would ever be happy again."

A tear began to fall from her left eye and Aaron almost dropped the armful of books to wipe it away.

"I'm sorry." She looked embarrassed and quickly reached up to wipe away the moisture from her face. "I know you've been through a lot; I don't want to make you feel any worse."

The nine-fifteen bell began to ring and the empty hallway was filled with its jarring, metallic peal.

"What I'm trying to say, Aaron, is that it won't hurt like this forever. Right now you probably don't think so, but trust me on this, okay?"

He nodded and tried to smile. "Thanks," he said as the corridor crowded with students going from one class to the next. "I really appreciate it."

He started to move away from his locker, from her. He had to go now or there was a good chance that he would never leave.

"I have . . . I have to go," he stammered, backing away.

She started to follow. "Where will you go?"

"I don't know," he answered truthfully. "I . . . I just have to get away." He had to find his brother and something inside was urging him to travel north. Camael said that it would be in their best interest to trust these urges.

Aaron started to turn away from her.

"Will you be back?" she asked hopefully, now at his side.

He shook his head. "No. I doubt it," he said, and looked away from her with feigned indifference. This was killing him. He hated to be so mean, but it was for her own good.

Aaron again heard Verchiel's cold words threatening to kill everyone close to him.

"I really have to go," he said, and quickened his pace, leaving her behind.

She moved in front of him, blocking his path, leaned in close, and took him in her arms. She smelled incredible, clean, like bath powder and fresh-cut flowers. She gave him a hug and a warm, gentle peck on the cheek that made his legs begin to tremble.

"You take care, Aaron Corbet," she said softly in his ear. "I'll miss you very much."

And he felt his heart shatter into a million, razor-sharp pieces that tore his insides to ribbons.

He didn't say anything more, forcing himself down the hall. After turning in his books at the main office, he practically ran from the building.

Outside on the steps, the wind blew and Aaron pulled the collar of his leather jacket up around his neck. Although it was officially spring, there was still a cruel bite of winter in the air. He was parked in the school's horseshoe-shaped driveway, and could see Camael and Gabriel waiting for him by the car.

This is it, he thought, and put his hands inside his pockets for warmth as he began to descend the steps.

Something was in one of his pockets, something that hadn't been there before.

He removed the piece of folded paper and opened it. It was from Vilma and it was her e-mail address and telephone number. She must have put it there when she hugged him. At the bottom of the paper, in delicate handwriting, it said, "Just in case you want to talk."

Aaron thought about throwing the paper away, but couldn't bring himself to do it. He placed it safely back inside his pocket and continued on his way to the car. For some reason, he felt strangely warmer.

He could hear Camael and Gabriel talking as he approached.

"For the last time, no," he heard the angel say, a touch of petulance in his tone.

"What's the problem?" Aaron asked as he came around the side of the car.

Gabriel had dropped the tennis ball at Camael's feet, and Aaron knew immediately what the problem was.

"He won't throw the ball for me, Aaron. I asked him nicely and he still refused. I think he's mean."

The angel seethed. "I have never thrown a ball and have no desire to ever do so. It has nothing to do with my temperament."

Aaron squatted down to the dog's level. "What did I tell you about trying to force people to play with you?"

The dog playfully swatted the ball with his paw and caught it in his mouth before it could roll away.

"Gabriel?" he cautioned.

The dog lowered his head, shamed by his master's disapproval. *"He wasn't doing anything, and I got bored."*

"He said he didn't want to play and you should respect that."

"I'm sorry, Aaron," Gabriel said, ears flat against his head.

Aaron lovingly ruffled the dog's floppy ears. "That's all right. Let's just try and be a little more considerate." Then he shot a withering look at the angel. "Though it probably wouldn't have killed you to toss the ball a couple of times."

"I still think he's mean," the dog muttered beneath his breath before he defiantly snatched up the ball in his mouth.

"Did you accomplish your task?" Camael asked, ignoring the animal, hands clasped behind his back.

Aaron turned and looked back at the school, taking in every detail of the brick and concrete structure. "Yeah," he said, saving the image of his high school to memory. "I'm ready to go."

He was opening the driver-side door of the car when Gabriel let out a cry.

"Shotgun!" he bellowed, startling them as he scrambled to the front, passenger-side door.

Camael looked at him, an expression of confusion on his goateed face. "What did you say?" he asked the dog.

"I said shotgun," Gabriel explained. *"It's what you're supposed to say when you want to ride in the front seat."*

Aaron could not help but laugh. No matter how many conversations he had with the animal, Gabriel's increased intelligence still managed to surprise him.

"That's what I thought you said," Aaron said. He then looked to Camael. "Do you mind riding in the back?"

"Front or back," Camael growled with an air of distaste. "It doesn't matter. I despise the confines of these hellish contraptions no matter where I ride."

"Great," Aaron said as he pulled open his door and pushed the driver's seat forward so that the angel could crawl into the back. Then he went around to the front passenger door to let his best friend in. "Shotgun is all yours," he told Gabriel, and let the dog hop up into the copilot seat.

"Awesome," said the dog, bright pink tongue lolling happily from his mouth as he panted with anticipation.

Aaron started to close the door. "Watch your tail," he said, and slammed the door closed.

He plopped himself down behind the wheel and started the car up, but did not put it into drive.

Aaron was staring at the school again—his school—and thought about all the things lost to him over the past few days: the closest thing to mother and father he had ever known, his home, his job, his school—and even his humanity.

He thought about Vilma, her eyes red from crying. If only he could have explained; yet another thing taken away from him.

"Are we ready, Aaron?" Camael asked impatiently from the back.

Aaron used the rearview mirror to look into the backseat and the angel seated there.

"To be perfectly honest, no, I'm not," he said, putting the car into drive. "But, from what you've told me about the prophecy and all, I don't think I really have much of a choice."

He pulled the car away from the curb and proceeded down the driveway. At the end of the drive he waited for his chance to go, and pulled out into the flow of traffic, pointing the car to the north and the uncertainty of the future, the still-tender memories of things loved and lost left sadly behind.

"Where are we going, Aaron?" Gabriel asked, his head moving excitedly from side to side as he watched the other cars on the road with them.

"I'm not sure," he answered, changing lanes to pass a minivan in need of a new exhaust system.

"Then how will we know when we get there?" the dog asked, concerned.

Aaron could feel the animal staring at him, waiting for an answer. He reached over and scratched beneath the dog's neck. "Don't worry pally," he said, keeping his eyes on the road. "I have a feeling we'll know."

It's supposed to be like this, he thought with disdain as he took the exit that would lead them onto the highway going north.

Predestined, whether he liked it or not.

The Saint Athanasius Church and Orphanage, vacant since 1959, squatted dark and brooding at the end of a seldom used road in western Massachusetts.

It was supposed to have been turned into elderly housing sometime in the mid-eighties, but the cost of refurbishing and renovating the buildings far exceeded their value.

There was an air of disquiet about the place, as if the old, ramshackle structures had gained sentience, and were bitter about being abandoned. It was this atmosphere that gave the grounds its reputation of being haunted.

So there it sat for the last forty-some years, its structure slowly wasting away at the mercy of the elements, absent of life except for the wild creatures of the fields that had gradually found their way inside the buildings, to live within the walls and nest in the belfry.

Mournfully vacant—until a few days ago.

From a wooden seat upon the altar within the Church of Saint Athanasius, Verchiel gazed up at the rounded, water-stained ceiling and examined the depiction of Heaven painted there.

The angel shifted uncomfortably in his chair as he studied the artwork. Pieces of burned flesh painfully flaked away from his body and fell to the altar floor.

"You haven't the slightest idea," he mused aloud as he gazed at the castle of gold floating among the clouds, and the harp-wielding angels that blissfully circled above it.

Kraus, the healer, crept carefully toward him, his worn leather satchel of medical tools wedged beneath his arm. Though blind, he stopped before Verchiel's chair, sensing his presence—his divinity—as only the imperfect could.

"I am here to minister to your needs, Great Verchiel," Kraus said, bowing his head in reverence.

Verchiel had been in perpetual agony since the lightning strike, the entire surface of his body charred black. "Proceed," he said with a wave of his blackened hand, his nerve endings vibrating in blinding pain with even the slightest movement.

The healer knelt down before Verchiel. He placed the satchel upon the ground, undid the tie, and rolled it open to expose the instruments contained within. His hands hovered over the wide variety of scalpels, blades, and saws—tools of healing used by his predecessor and hundreds of others before him.

By touch he found what was needed, a twelve-inch blade that glinted sharply in the beams of sunlight that streamed in through openings in the boarded-up windows.

"Shall we proceed?" the human monkey asked, the sourness of his breath offensive to Verchiel's heightened senses.

The quicker he was treated, the quicker he could be away from the offensive animal. "Do as you must," Verchiel responded. He lifted one of his arms and presented it to the healer, a sound like dry leaves rustling in the wind filled the air.

The healer leaned forward, and with great

skill, began to cut away the burned, dead flesh.

The pain was unbearable, but Verchiel did not cry out, for it was part of the price he must pay. What was it when the monkeys begged forgiveness for their indiscretions?

Doing penance, he believed it was called.

It was obvious that he had disappointed his Holy Master, for why else would he have been punished so? The pain was his penance. For failing to slay the false prophet he had to suffer, to show that he was truly sorry.

Kraus carefully peeled away a swath of dead skin to expose the raw, moist flesh beneath. If he was to eventually heal, this would need to be done to his entire body; all the burned, dead skin would need to be removed. It would be a long, painful process, but it was something Verchiel was willing to endure—the penance he would pay to receive the Creator's forgiveness.

The sound of a child's moan distracted him from his agony.

The Nephilim's brother, the imperfect one called Stevie, sat on the far side of the altar and rocked from side to side, staring wide-eyed at what had been placed before him.

It was a helmet the rich color of blood, cast in the forges of Heaven—a gift to the child from his new master.

The child groaned again, his eyes transfixed upon it, almost as if he were somehow cognizant of the fate he, and it, would eventually share.

"I shall change you, my pet," Verchiel said with a hiss, his body trembling with torment as more of his skin was cut away. A pile of dead flesh grew at his feet as the healer continued his gruesome task.

"Transforming you into my hunter of false prophets—"

The child rocked from side to side, his repetitive cries of "no" echoing through the once holy place.

"A tool of absolution," Verchiel said as he leaned his head back against the chair and again looked to the church ceiling and the all too human images of Paradise. A place that, if he were to have his way, only the truly worthy would ever be allowed to enter.

"My instrument of redemption."